To my son and daughter
with all my prayers
and all my love

Always, Mom

With This Ring

ROBIN JONES GUNN

BETHANY HOUSE PUBLISHERS
MINNEAPOLIS, MINNESOTA 55438

With This Ring
Copyright © 1997
Robin Jones Gunn

Edited by Janet Kobobel Grant
Cover illustration by George Angelini
Cover design by Praco, Ltd.

Augustine quotation on page 115 is from *Inspiring Quotations, Contemporary and Classical,* compiled by Albert M. Wells, Jr. (Nashville: Thomas Nelson, 1988), p. 76, #962.

Scripture quotations are from the New King James Version of the Bible. Copyright © 1979, 1980, 1982, by Thomas Nelson, Inc., Publishers. Used by permission. All rights reserved.

A Focus on the Family book published by
Bethany House Publishers
A Ministry of Bethany Fellowship International
11400 Hampshire Avenue South, Minneapolis, Minnesota 55438
www.bethanyhouse.com

Printed in the United States of America by
Bethany Press International, Minneapolis, Minnesota 55438

Library of Congress Cataloging-in-Publication Data

Gunn, Robin Jones, 1955–
    With this ring / Robin Jones Gunn.
       p. cm. — (The Sierra Jensen series ; #6)
    Summary: While attending a wedding with friends, sixteen-year-old Sierra understands the value of sexual abstinence and promises God that she will save herself for marriage.
     ISBN 1–56179–540–2
    [1. Sexual abstinence—Fiction. 2. Weddings—Fiction.
3. Self-esteem—Fiction. 4. Christian life—Fiction.] I. Title.
II. Series: Gunn, Robin Jones, 1955–   . Sierra Jensen series ; #6.
PZ7.G972Whj 1997
[Fic]—dc21
                                        97–9
                                        CIP
                                        AC

00 01 02 03 04 / 15 14 13 12 11 10 9 8 7

Chapter One

WITH ONE LAST GLANCE IN HER BEDROOM mirror, Sierra Jensen slipped a silver bracelet on her arm and called out, "Mom, tell him I'll be there in a second."

Sierra wondered if she should change into jeans. The short dress she now wore was a little too fancy for her. But this July night in Portland was hot, and the thought of jeans sounded uncomfortable. A dress was the way to go. But maybe not this dark, straight dress. What about a long, gauze skirt?

Sierra began to rifle through the volcano of clothes that had erupted in the middle of her bed.

Where is that blue skirt? she wondered. *I saw it a few minutes ago when I was looking for my other shoe. Oh, yeah, under the bed.*

For a few weeks after Sierra's older sister had moved out, Sierra had kept her room neat. Then, as summer progressed and she became busier, the clutter seemed to expand to fill any empty space it could find within her bedroom. More than once Sierra had set out to clean the messy room, but the weeks of junk buildup had turned it from a one-hour cleanup to an all-day-with-a-shovel event. So she kept putting it off.

Bending down, Sierra lifted the dust ruffle. A half-eaten graham cracker greeted her, along with two cotton balls, a pair of socks, a magazine, a ponytail holder that had turned into a dust-ball magnet, and her A+ essay on Marie Antoinette. No blue skirt.

"Sierra!" Mrs. Jensen's voice came from above Sierra. "What are you doing?"

Pulling herself out from her unladylike position under the bed, Sierra faced her mom. Sierra's wild, wavy blond hair had flopped across her face. "I didn't hear you come in," she said.

Sierra's Granna Mae stood behind her mom. Both of them were smiling. Sharon Jensen, a trim woman in her forties, looked more like an older sister than the mother of six children.

"It's not polite to keep a man waiting," Granna Mae said. "Are you ready to go, Lovey?"

"I guess," Sierra said, straightening her dress and smoothing back her hair. "I was thinking of changing into a long skirt."

"You look fine," her mother said. "He's taking you to a nice restaurant, you know. You wouldn't want to dress too casually."

"I know. But I feel so silly about this," Sierra confessed. "I don't know why he asked me to go out to dinner with him."

"You don't have any idea?" her mom asked.

"No, but I suppose you do."

"Maybe," her mom said with a smile in her eyes.

"Okay, I'm ready. I just wish you guys weren't all making such a big deal out of this."

"You've become quite the young lady," Granna Mae said. "You'll certainly turn his head tonight."

Sierra impulsively gave her grandma a peck on the cheek as Sierra swished past her and headed down the stairs of their large Victorian home.

"I think you two are enjoying this milestone in my dating life more than I am."

She felt her cheeks beginning to blush when she noticed her date standing in the hallway by the front door.

He had on a sports jacket and dress slacks. The faint scent of his evergreen aftershave rose to meet her. He turned to watch her coming down the stairs, and Sierra could see he held a clear plastic box tied with a purple ribbon.

I can't believe he bought me a corsage! This is getting way too corny. What if I tell him I've changed my mind and don't want to go after all?

"You look beautiful." His deep voice was soothing. Sierra looked up into his familiar, clean-shaven face, framed by short brown hair with a receding hairline. The corners of his eyes crinkled up the way they always did when he was trying not to cry.

"Dad," Sierra said softly, "I know this is supposed to be some kind of special father-daughter event, but I really feel lame dressing up and going out to dinner. If you want to tell me something, can't we just go in the study or out to your workshop?"

"This is for you," her dad said, unaffected by her attempt to squelch their plans. "I had them make it into a wrist corsage because I didn't know if you would want to wear it on your dress."

Sierra looked down at the small corsage of delicate pink baby rosebuds. She recognized the name of the flower shop on the gold sticker. ZuZu's Petals. It was just down the street from Mama Bear's Bakery, where Sierra worked. She had applied for a job once at ZuZu's Petals and found that the owner knew Granna Mae. Now they probably knew her father. Did he tell them why he was buying the corsage?

"Maybe I should leave this here in the refrigerator," Sierra said cautiously as she took the box from him. "They're so pretty. I'd hate to squash them."

Her dad looked disappointed. Then he said, "Well, it's up to you. They're yours."

A tiny card peeped out from the top of the box. Sierra flipped it open with her thumb and read her dad's message. "You will always be my daughter, and I will always love you. Dad."

Sierra bit her lower lip and tasted the lip gloss she had put on 15 minutes earlier. How could she reject the flowers? Even though she didn't understand what this father-daughter bonding night was about, Sierra knew she couldn't leave his corsage in the refrigerator.

"It's really beautiful," she said with a catch in her throat. "Thanks, Dad. I'll take it with us."

"Good. You all ready then?"

Mrs. Jensen, who had been hanging back at the top of the stairs, called down, "Wait a minute, you two! I need to take a picture."

Sierra forced a smile as her mom scurried down the stairs.

This is going to be a long night! she thought. *I hope we don't see anyone I know.*

"Okay," Mrs. Jensen said, squeezing one eye shut and holding the camera steady. "Put your arms around each other. That's good. Come on, Sierra, smile. Okay, hold that!"

The camera clicked, and immediately Sierra's mom said, "Wait! I want to get a close-up now."

Tucking her short blond hair behind her ears, Sharon Jensen coerced them into posing again.

"Bye now," she said after the camera clicked once more. "Have a great time, and remember, Howard, my daughter needs to be back by her curfew."

"Yes, ma'am," he said, opening the door for Sierra.

They headed for her brother Wesley's new sports car. It was actually an old sports car, a 1969 Triumph, that Wes had bought almost a month ago. He and Mr. Jensen had spent hours fixing it up, and now, according to them, the little baby "hummed." Sierra was glad her brother was working tonight and hadn't been there to tease her.

"I thought you might find this a little more appealing

than the family van," her dad said as he started up the engine. "Ah! Purrs like a kitten." He pulled out of the driveway and headed down their quiet street.

This part of Portland was known for its rows of restored Victorian homes. Sierra's grandfather had built the one they lived in, and many of the original owners or their families still resided along this tree-lined street.

"So, where are we going?" Sierra asked.

"I thought I'd keep it a surprise," her dad said.

He headed toward the Burnside Bridge that would take them over the Willamette River and into downtown Portland.

Sierra glanced at the corsage box in her lap and noticed how short her skirt was. She tried to tug it down a bit. Funny, it didn't seem short when she bought it or when she put it on this evening. But now, sitting next to her dad, Sierra wished she had changed into the long gauze skirt.

"How are things going at the Highland House?" her dad asked.

"Great. Did I tell you about the macaroni necklaces?"

"No. I noticed the kitchen was full of bowls of dyed macaroni last week. What did you do with it?"

"I had no idea the kids at the homeless shelter would get so into making necklaces. I took all the macaroni and let them string their own bracelets and necklaces, and they went crazy! Some of them did a really good job. I told the older girls I'd bring beads for them next week."

"Your mom and I are proud of the way you've been helping out there this summer and keeping up with your job at Mama Bear's. You've been busy."

"It's been a good summer," Sierra said, slowly removing the corsage from the box in her lap. The pink rosebuds trembled as she lifted them to her nose. There was only a slight fragrance. The mist clinging to the roses and feathery fern leaves dotted the end of her nose with moisture.

"And the summer isn't over yet," Sierra said, dabbing her nose with the back of her hand. "I'm really looking forward to going to California next week."

Maybe I can carry the flowers into the restaurant without anyone seeing them and keep them beside my plate, she thought. *It would sure make Dad happy.*

The car came to a stop, and Sierra looked up. *Oh no!* she inwardly groaned.

"Here we are," her dad said.

Not here! Please, Dad! Of all the restaurants in Portland, why did you have to pick this one?

Chapter Two

"*I*'VE HEARD YOU AND WES TALK ABOUT THIS place so much that I thought it would be fun if we checked it out," Mr. Jensen said as he opened the door for Sierra.

She forced a smile and carefully held on to the corsage. She tried to get out of the sardine-can sports car without her short skirt hiking up and her hair falling in her face. She found it to be a difficult task.

"May I offer you a hand?" her father said gallantly.

"No, I'm fine," Sierra said. She pushed herself up and out, trying to appear graceful. Fortunately, no one was in the parking lot, watching her.

Offering Sierra his arm, Mr. Jensen prepared to escort her into the Italian restaurant that was owned by the uncle of Sierra's friend Amy. Amy worked there as a hostess, and she had arranged for a lot of their friends to get jobs there. Wes was a waiter; he was working tonight. Sierra felt certain her dad was so into this that he probably had arranged for Wes to wait on them. Her buddy Randy was a busboy, and so was Tre, another guy from school who played in a band with Randy.

Sierra barely touched her dad's arm as they walked into the restaurant together. What would people think if they saw this 16-year-old girl, all dressed up—with a corsage, no less—being ushered into a nice restaurant by a middle-aged man with a receding hairline who was grinning from ear to ear? This was so embarrassing.

Her dad opened the door for her, which gave her an opportunity to let go of his arm and walk slightly away from him. A dozen people were seated on antique benches, waiting for open tables.

The first person Sierra noticed when they entered was Amy. She had on the lace vest she had bought two days ago when she and Sierra were out vintage-store shopping. It looked cute over her navy dress. Her long black hair was pulled back with one tendril cascading down the right side of her face. Amy had a glimmer in her dark eyes that indicated to Sierra that she knew about this father-daughter date and had been expecting them.

"Good evening," Amy said formally. She made a mark on the seating chart in front of her. "Reservation for Jensen, party of two. Right this way, please."

Sierra fell in line behind her friend and whispered, "Okay, Amy, cut the act. This is humiliating enough without you playing along."

"Who's playing along?" Amy whispered over her shoulder as they wound past the round tables in the packed restaurant. "This is what I do every night."

Sierra wanted to playfully pinch her friend, but before

she could, Amy turned, and with wide eyes, she whispered to Sierra, "There he is. Over there by table 17. That's Nathan. Is he a dream or what?"

"Table 17? Where's that? I don't see any dream."

"Over there," Amy said under her breath. "By the window. He asked me tonight if I have to work next Tuesday."

"Oh," Sierra said.

Amy had been raving about this guy for the last two weeks, ever since he had started to work there. That was about the same time Amy had given up trying to snag Sierra's brother. Wes was nice to Amy, and she had hoped all summer for something more. But when nothing happened and Nathan came to work at the restaurant, Amy quickly readjusted her goal.

Sierra glanced at Amy's new dream boy again. Nathan looked as if he were about 20. He had bleached blond hair that was combed straight back and dark eyebrows over deep-set eyes. His severe looks didn't appeal to Sierra. She knew he had really made an impression on Amy, though.

Amy stopped at a booth in the back corner of the restaurant and motioned for Sierra to slide in.

"Don't you get it?" Amy whispered. "Tuesday is Nathan's night off. I think he's going to ask me out!"

She handed Sierra a menu and then handed one to Sierra's dad.

Clearing her throat and switching back to her hostess voice, Amy said, "Wesley will be your server tonight. He'll be here in a moment to tell you about our specials. Enjoy your dinner."

Amy gave Sierra a little raised-eyebrow gesture, and as Sierra watched, Amy walked the long way back to the front of the restaurant just so she would have to walk past table 17, where Nathan was writing down an order. He turned his head slightly as she passed, and Sierra knew Amy's guess was probably right. She had attracted his attention, and he would undoubtedly ask her out.

The whole scenario didn't feel right to Sierra. Maybe the unsettled feeling came from watching Amy's dating life unfold while Sierra sat with her "daddy," trying to find a way to hide her rosebud corsage. She placed it next to her fork, then unfolded the cloth napkin and laid it in her lap. Sierra realized she owed it to her dad to be appreciative of all this attention. He had obviously gone to a lot of effort.

"Hi," Wes said, stepping up to the table. He was a younger version of their dad in many ways, including his lean build and clear brown eyes that crinkled in the corners when he laughed. The biggest difference between the two was that Wes had a full head of wavy brown hair.

Pulling out his notepad, Wes asked, "Would you like to hear about our specials?"

Mr. Jensen closed his menu and said, "Why don't you give us your expert recommendation."

Sierra felt relieved that Wes hadn't done anything to tease her. In a way, it felt as if they were a bunch of little kids playing grown-ups.

"The manicotti is superb tonight. That's what I had on my break. You might want an antipasto salad and an order of Tony's Romano bread, too. The bread is our house specialty and is made with bits of tomato and melted cheese on top."

"Sounds good to me," Mr. Jensen said. "What would you like, Sierra?"

"That sounds good to me, too. Just a small salad, though. And I'd like some mineral water."

"I'll have water and coffee," her dad said.

Wes's pencil scratched across the notepad. He picked up the menus and gave his dad and sister a nod as if they were any other customers on any other night. "Very good. I'll get those drinks right out for you."

As Wes walked away, Randy, who was busing the table next to theirs, stepped over. He held a tubful of dishes and had a white apron tied around his waist. She hadn't seen him in the white-shirt-and-black-bow-tie uniform before. The waiter outfit looked normal on Wes; but Randy, with his crooked smile and chin-length, straight blond hair parted down the middle, looked as if he were dressed for a costume party.

"Hey, Sierra! Hey, Mr. J.! Did you hear about Drake's accident?" Randy said.

"No. What happened? Is he okay?"

"Yeah. He was driving the delivery truck and hit a phone pole. Blew out the front tire. It was over in Laurelhurst, and I was there doing lawns. I heard this huge crash and ran down the block to see what it was, and there was Drake. The engine was smoking. He was pretty ticked. He said he swerved to miss a cat."

Sierra knew how her dad felt about cats and was hoping he wouldn't throw out a comment about how it would have been better to rid the world of that cat than to crash because of it.

Fortunately, Mr. Jensen only said, "What kind of delivery truck?"

"Bundle of Joy," Randy said, readjusting his posture so that the dishes rattled slightly.

"It's his dad's business," Sierra explained.

"Bundle of Joy diapers?" her dad asked.

Sierra nodded. She knew what he was thinking. Anyone who met tall, dark, and athletic Drake would never picture him driving a diaper delivery truck.

One of the other waiters came up behind Randy and said, "Table seven, and can you hurry?"

"Gotta go," Randy said. He turned, and then with a quick look over his shoulder, he added, "You look real nice, Sierra."

"Thanks," she murmured, feeling a tinge of pink rising up from her neck.

"You have great friends," her dad said after Randy disappeared.

"I know I do." Sierra thought how nice it was that Randy had been so comfortable around her. She and Randy had seen each other nearly every day this summer. At the beginning of the summer, they had acted as if they were dating. Then, after an adventurous backpacking trip, they had settled back into their "just buddies" relationship, and everything had felt normal since then.

Sierra had considered dating Drake for a while, too. They did go out to the movies once, just the two of them. But when everything had started to unravel in her other friendships, Sierra decided she wasn't ready to exclusively date one guy. Her other friendships were too important to her. Drake had said he understood, but he didn't pursue her too much after that. As interested as he said he was on their first date, he cooled off when things didn't continue on the course he had set.

Wes brought the drinks and a warm plate of Tony's Romano bread. Sierra began feeling a little more comfortable and settled into this evening with her dad. The scent of garlic immediately piqued her appetite.

"Are your plans all set for next week? When do you leave?" Mr. Jensen asked.

"I fly down to Orange County on Wednesday afternoon. Tawni is going to pick me up."

"And who is it that's getting married?"

"Doug and Tracy."

"Oh, right. He was the group leader on your outreach trip to England last January."

Sierra nodded. "And he's friends with Jeremy." She wasn't sure if her dad remembered the connection between Doug and Tawni's boyfriend. "Jeremy and Tawni are going to the wedding, too."

"Right. I think I remember hearing that. Sounds like a fun week for you." Her dad sipped his coffee.

"I'm ready for it," Sierra said. "Did you know I worked 42 hours last week at Mama Bear's? Everyone decided to go on vacation at the same time. Mrs. Kraus was great about letting me have the time off. She has a new person coming in to train while I'm gone since I'll have to go back to my 12 hours a week when school starts."

"Here you are," Wes said, placing the salads before them in bright blue-and-white Italian pottery bowls. "Would either of you care for grated cheese on your salad?"

"No thanks."

"Not for me."

"Enjoy!" Wes said, walking away with the cheese grater in his hand.

"Would you like to pray with me?" Mr. Jensen asked Sierra. He always prayed when they ate out, so it seemed natural to Sierra. She bowed her head and closed her eyes while her dad thanked God for the food and for his beautiful daughter.

When he said, "Amen," Sierra looked up and said, "Thanks, Dad."

He gave her a little wink, and they started on their salads.

Sierra had hardly swallowed her first bite when her dad said, "I guess you're wondering why I asked you out like this."

For some reason, Sierra's heart began to pound again. She lowered her fork and waited to hear what her dad had to say.

Chapter Three

"YOU KNOW," MR. JENSEN BEGAN, clearing his throat twice, "ever since you told your mom and me a couple months ago that you were going to write out your goals and standards for dating, we've been talking about what we could do to encourage you."

Sierra slowly took a bite of her salad and waited for him to continue.

"That's what I wanted to do tonight," her dad said, clearing his throat again. It seemed to Sierra that he was a little nervous about all this, too. "I wanted to find a way to show you how special you are. Not only to your mother and me, but to God."

Sierra nodded. "Thanks, Dad, I appreciate that. But you don't have to do all this to make me feel special."

Mr. Jensen munched his salad. He seemed to be thinking. Either that or trying not to look nervous. This was all a little awkward. She knew her parents loved her, and she knew God loved her. But the ceremony of dressing up and going out to dinner seemed like overkill.

"I'd like to know what you ended up writing out," her father said. "Your goals and standards, I mean. What's on your list?"

"I'm not sure I remember. I mean, I remember, but not the exact words. I wrote two different lists. One is sort of like my criteria for the kind of guy I'd go out with, and the other list, I guess you could say, is my creed."

"Your creed. Sounds interesting. I'd like to hear about both of them."

"Well," Sierra said, putting down her fork and pushing her nearly finished salad to the end of the table, "I only had three points on the boyfriend list."

"Yes?"

"The first one was that he has to be a Christian. And not just a believer but a really strong, growing Christian. A God-lover."

"A God-lover?"

Sierra nodded. "That's what Doug and Jeremy and their friends call themselves."

"I like that."

"So do I," Sierra said. "The next requirement, or whatever, is that he has plans to serve God with his life. I think what I wrote down is that he's committed to God and is planning to serve God in his future career."

"Are you saying you only want to date future pastors or missionaries?"

"No, that's not what I mean," Sierra said. "You don't have to be a pastor to put God at the center of your work. Like with Doug. He's an assistant to a financial planner.

He'll probably be a businessman all his life because that's where his strengths are. But Christy told me that he and Tracy are budgeting to live on half his income so they can give the other half to missionaries."

"Really?" her dad said, raising his eyebrows.

"I don't know if they'll be able to do it or not," Sierra said. "But I like it that Doug puts God at the center of his career, and even though he's getting married, his goals don't change."

"Quite noble," her dad said.

Wesley arrived at the table with plates of steaming manicotti and placed them before Sierra and her dad. "Some grated Romano for either of you?"

"No thanks," Sierra said.

"Sure, I'll take a spin," said her dad.

Wes twisted the handle of the fancy cheese grater and the thin white flakes floated down.

"That's good," Mr. Jensen said.

"I'll be back with more coffee," Wes said. He looked at Sierra and then at her right hand. With a glance at Mr. Jensen, he turned and left.

"Go on," Sierra's dad urged. "Any guy you date must be a God-lover who is planning to honor God with his career. What else?"

Sierra felt a little embarrassed telling her dad this one. She sunk her fork into the soft pasta and said, "Well, I guess the way I wrote it down was that I have to be attracted to him and vice-versa. And that we're both committed to saving ourselves physically for our future mate."

"Sounds as if you have some pretty serious and stiff guidelines."

Sierra was surprised. She took another bite of the delicious dinner and then asked, "Do you think my goals are too high or something?"

"Oh, no! They're terrific. I can tell you've really thought it through. What about the other list? Your creed. I take it you mean a creed as in a summary of what you believe."

Sierra nodded.

"Where did you come up with that idea?"

"You're going to laugh."

"Try me."

"I saw this poster in a music store at the mall when I was there with Randy a couple of months ago. It was called 'The Rocker's Creed,' and it had a list of 10 points for people who believe in hard rock. It was supposed to be funny. Like, 'If it's too loud, you're too old.'"

Her dad smiled.

"Well, my creed is what I believe about staying pure." Sierra took another bite and chewed slowly. She had felt so spiritual a few months ago when she wrote all this out. Now she felt silly and embarrassed talking about it with her dad. She knew she shouldn't feel that way, but she did.

"What does your creed say?"

"It just says that my body is a gift and that God gets to decide who to give the gift to, not me. And the best presents are the ones that are all wrapped up, not the ones that have been opened and rewrapped and now the paper is torn or the bow is squished or the tape no longer sticks. Do you know what I mean?"

Her dad was smiling softly, and his eyes were starting to get all crinkly in the corners. He nodded, urging her to continue.

"That's it, basically. I believe God's best plan is for me to be like a wrapped present. Then, when I get married, I can completely give myself to my husband for the first time, and he'll know that I'm a special gift just for him."

There. That wasn't so embarrassing. Why do I feel so self-conscious about all this? Sierra wondered.

A tear glistened in the corner of her dad's eye, and he tilted his head down, moving his manicotti around on his plate. Then, lifting his face, he said, "That's beautiful, honey. I could never have said it better. That's exactly what you are: a very special and wonderful gift. I'm proud of you."

Amy stepped up to their table and leaned toward Sierra, breaking the moment.

"Sierra, guess what?" Amy said breathlessly, her dark eyes dancing. "He asked me out! For Tuesday; just like I thought. We have to go shopping this weekend, Sierra! I have to get something new to wear."

"Okay," Sierra agreed. It was hard to switch into Amy's dreamworld when she and her dad were in the middle of this delicate conversation.

"Aren't you even excited for me?" Amy said.

"Yes, of course I am. That's great." Sierra wished she could really feel happy for her friend—Nathan didn't impress Sierra as exactly the catch of the day. But maybe she was jumping to conclusions.

"I'm so excited!" Amy said, giving Sierra's arm a squeeze before hurrying back to the hostess' station.

"Girl talk?" her dad asked.

"Yes. Sorry."

"No problem. I'm about ready for dessert. How about you?"

"Sure."

When Wes stopped by their table a few minutes later, they ordered the tiramisu based on his recommendation. Sierra also ordered herb tea and watched Nathan out of the corner of her eye.

"May I take those plates for you?" Randy reached for Sierra's plate and the empty bread plate. "Oh, you guys had Tony's bread. Good stuff, isn't it?"

"It was," Sierra agreed. "So was the manicotti."

"It looks good tonight," Randy said. "I get my break in 10 minutes, and I think that's what I'm going to have. I'll see you later."

With the table cleared, Sierra's dad brushed away a few crumbs and then pulled a piece of paper from inside his coat pocket. "I wrote down a few things," he said, "but I don't know if I need to say many of them since you've taken such a strong position on protecting your purity. I went to a men's group a couple of weeks ago; I don't know if you remember. Anyway, the challenge to us dads was to help direct our kids toward purity."

Sierra remembered how excited her dad had been after

that all-day meeting at church. Randy had said his dad had been, too. Now the dinner and this heart-to-heart conversation made sense. This was his assignment, or at least his challenge, from the men's meeting: to talk to his children about abstinence. Sierra hoped he wasn't going to list all the reasons for remaining sexually inactive the way her science teacher had last spring. She wasn't in the mood for a list of STDs right before dessert.

"The first thing on my list here," her dad began, "is that I want you to know we trust you and your judgment when it comes to relationships. But any time you have questions or doubts of any kind, I want you to come to your mother or to me. Okay? As your father, you can trust me with any-thing, no matter how embarrassing you might think it is."

"Okay," Sierra agreed.

"I mean that, now. You can always talk to your mother and me."

"I know," Sierra said.

"The next thing I want to say is that God's way is always the best way. It's the only way, really. And God's Word clearly says He created sex for one man and one woman to share only inside the commitment of marriage."

Sierra started to feel embarrassed again and wished her dad didn't have such a loud voice. She hoped the people next to them couldn't hear what he was saying.

"I have a verse here I wanted to read to you," her dad said, unfolding the piece of paper in his hands.

Sierra noticed all the tidy little letters lined up in out-line form, which was his typical way of writing. He even outlined grocery lists. His letters were all in capitals and always straight, even if there were no lines to follow. She could tell he had spent some time on this.

"1 Corinthians 6:19 says, 'Or do you not know that your body is the temple of the Holy Spirit who is in you, whom you have from God, and you are not your own?'" Mr. Jensen looked up from his notes and said, "Actually, that's just what you were saying. Your body is a gift, and it's up to God to decide who gets that gift."

Wesley approached them with a teapot in one hand and a scrumptious-looking chocolate-layered dessert in the other. "Tiramisu for two, cherry almond tea, and I'll be right back with some more coffee." He disappeared as quickly as he had come.

"Let me read you verse 20," her dad said. "'For you were bought at a price; therefore glorify God in your body and in your spirit, which are God's.'"

Sierra dunked the tea bag into the white pot and decided she didn't want her tea too strong.

"I know you believe this already," her father said.

"I do," Sierra replied.

"I'm proud of the way you've given yourself guidelines and written out your creed. I know from experience that being a virgin when you get married is the only way to go."

Sierra had heard her mom say before that she and her dad were virgins when they married. It sounded a little different coming from her father, though. Comforting. It gave her a sense of hope that maybe somewhere in the world, quality guys were saving themselves for their future wives.

Chapter Four

S IERRA SANK HER FORK INTO THE TEMPTING dessert and let the first bite melt in her mouth. "Oh, this is good," she said.

Mr. Jensen folded his page of notes and tucked the paper back into his pocket. As Sierra was digging in for a second bite, she noticed her dad was pulling a small black gift box from his inside pocket.

"This is for you," he said, placing the jewelry box in front of her. "Mom and I wanted you to have this. It's our way of supporting and affirming your choice to remain pure and to save yourself for your future husband."

Sierra quickly swallowed the bite in her mouth and looked up with surprise. "What is it?"

"Open it and see."

She lifted the hinged lid on the velvet-lined box. There, wedged in the padded slot, was a simple gold ring.

Gold!? I only wear silver. Why did they get me a gold ring?

"Look on the inside," her dad urged. His face was red with anticipation. Sierra didn't dare mention that she never wore anything gold.

Inside the thin band was engraved "1 Cor. 6:19–20."

"Those are the verses you read to me," Sierra said.

Mr. Jensen nodded enthusiastically. "It'll be a reminder to you always that you belong to God and that, as you said, your body is a gift that should stay wrapped until your wedding night."

"Thanks." Sierra didn't know what else to say.

"Try it on."

She wasn't sure on which hand such a ring should be worn. She decided to slip it onto the ring finger on her right hand. It somehow felt as if that was where it ought to be.

"It's nice," she said, giving her dad the smile he was waiting for. "Thank you."

"I'm glad you like it." He plunged his fork into the dessert before him.

Sierra glanced at the ring and then took another bite of dessert. It seemed strange to wear jewelry she hadn't selected for herself. And the gold was really going to take some time to get used to.

Wes returned with the check and looked at Sierra's hand again. He smiled at Mr. Jensen and said to Sierra, "Do you like it? I helped him pick it out."

"Yes. It's nice."

"Dad said you only liked silver, but I convinced him that the gold is what would set this ring apart. This way it doesn't look like costume jewelry. Makes it unique."

As Wes was speaking, Sierra noticed for the first time that he wore a similar gold band on his right hand. "When did you get that?" she asked, nodding at his ring.

"Last week when Dad got your ring. He bought one for Tawni, too."

"You and Dad went out on a 'date,' and I didn't hear about it?" Sierra teased.

"No. He gave me my ring in the car on the way back from the jeweler. Only you and Tawni get the special treatment." Wes picked up the small tray with the check and Mr. Jensen's credit card. "I'll be right back."

Sierra turned to her dad and asked, "When are you going to give Tawni her ring?"

"I'm not sure," he said, drawing in a deep breath. "I thought about having you take it to her next week when you go visit. It wouldn't be as special as this, of course, but I don't know when she'll be back up. Either that or I might just have to make a special trip down there."

"She would probably appreciate that," Sierra said. She didn't feel confident she would be able to deliver such a ring to her sister and that it would have the meaning it was supposed to.

Mr. Jensen signed the credit card voucher, and as he took his copy, Sierra noticed he left an extremely generous tip for Wes. He got up to go. Sierra scooped up her corsage and held it more confidently as they walked through the restaurant.

As they were about to exit, Randy came up and said, "Are you going to the Highland House tomorrow?"

"No, not until Monday. I work all day tomorrow."

"Me, too," Randy said. His job busing tables was only

two nights a week, but he also had a lawn-care business that kept him busy five and sometimes six days a week. "I'll see you later," he said before hustling off to clear more tables.

Amy pulled Sierra to the side before they left the restaurant. A throng of people were in the waiting area. "Call me tomorrow morning before you go to work, okay? I was thinking I wouldn't have to buy anything new if I could borrow your blue gauze skirt. It would go with that crushed velvet top I just bought."

"You can borrow it," Sierra said. "Only you'll have to come over and help me dig for it. My room is a mess."

"I know what you mean. I haven't been home long enough to clean mine."

"That's the excuse I keep using, too," Sierra said. "I'll call you."

Sierra's dad held the door open for her, and they strolled to the parking lot. She didn't feel nearly as embarrassed as she had going in. She wished she had worn the corsage, just to make her dad happy.

"You know, I hope you don't lose any of your spunk," her dad said.

"Lose any of my spunk?"

"I'm just saying you have your own style. Your own charm and vivacity. I just hope you always keep that when it comes to your relationships with guys."

He opened the car door and Sierra got in, carefully pulling on her short skirt to keep it down.

"Are you afraid I won't?" Sierra asked once her dad

was in the car. "I mean, that I won't keep being myself around guys?"

"No, I believe you will always be yourself no matter whom you're around. That's one of your strong suits. I guess what I'm trying to say is that you have some pretty high standards, and I support all of your goals 100 percent."

"But . . . ," Sierra nudged him on.

"Just don't forget you're a teenager. You're supposed to have fun during this time. You can keep all your virtue intact and still enjoy yourself. That's all I'm trying to say. Don't get too serious, thinking that any guy you go out with is on trial as future husband material. Relax and enjoy the chance to make a lot of friends. God will bring the right man into your life at the right time."

Sierra took her dad's words to heart and wrote them out, as best as she could remember them, in her journal that night. Her dad was right. She needed to have fun, too, and not always feel as if she were scoping out every guy to see how spiritual he was.

Closing her journal and snapping off the light, Sierra snuggled under the cool sheets. She felt her new ring with her thumb and twisted it around her ring finger. It felt smooth and light.

Outside her open window, a frog had joined the chorus of nightly cricket chirpers. The warm summer breeze ruffled her sheer bedroom curtains, making them look like dancing spirits in the glow of the streetlight below.

Her thoughts floated to Paul. For many months, she had prayed for him. At the end of the school year, her brief dreams of a romance with him were dashed when he had the nerve to ask if she had a crush on him.

What Sierra felt for Paul Mackenzie did not fall into the "crush" category. It was something so deep, she didn't even know what to call it. Maybe it was the intense spiritual connection she felt from all the times she had prayed for him. Or maybe it was nothing but an illusion she had allowed herself to entertain for too long. Sierra knew she was capable of talking herself into anything— even into believing there still was something between her and Paul.

But she had no pinch of evidence that he was interested in her. In many ways, Sierra was better off forgetting all about him. It made much more sense to pour her emotional energy into her friendship with Randy. That was a relationship with genuine openness and honesty. A friendship of daylight and solid evidence, not one of fleeting wishes and dreams in the night.

The hardest thing for Sierra was that she didn't feel she could talk about these things with Amy or anyone else. The only friend who would understand was Christy. She would see Christy next week, and hopefully the two of them could have a real heart-to-heart. Christy seemed to understand about holding someone in your heart, not only because she was older than Sierra, but also because Christy had found the true love of her life—Todd. They were waiting for God's direction in their relationship.

Christy was the person Sierra admired and wanted to imitate.

She fell asleep praying for Paul and for his time in Scotland, that going to school and visiting his grandmother would be full of rich spiritual growth. The thousands of miles between them couldn't stop her thoughts from reaching out to Paul. And she knew nothing could stop her prayers for him.

Chapter Five

AMY CAME BY SUNDAY EVENING, STILL excited about her date with Nathan and still determined to borrow Sierra's blue skirt. The two of them hunted through Sierra's bedroom for half an hour. Actually, Sierra hunted while Amy sat in the overstuffed chair and chattered endlessly about Nathan.

"I found out at work last night that Nathan loves peanut butter cookies. So I thought I would make some for him as a surprise on Tuesday night. Did I tell you he moved here from Seattle? He says it's hotter here in the summer than in Seattle. Hey, is that it? Right there under the jeans. That's your blue skirt."

"You're right," Sierra said. "This is so ridiculous. I should have been hanging up this stuff while I was looking. Here you go. It's a wrinkled mess, but you can borrow it. If you decide to wash it, make sure you do it by hand in cold water, then wring it out and let it hang dry."

"It doesn't look dirty to me. Isn't it supposed to be wrinkled? I think it's perfect." Amy admired the skirt, then turned to Sierra. "So, are you getting excited about your vacation?"

31

"I don't know if it's really a vacation. I guess it sort of is. But I'm definitely looking forward to it." Sierra opened her closet door and pulled out a few hangers for her clothes.

"I'd better go," Amy said. "It's after 9:00 already, and Nathan might call." She stood and turned her ear to the open window, listening. "Is that a frog?"

"Yes. He showed up a few nights ago. I guess he's trying to compete with all those crickets. Their concert last night kept me awake."

"They are pretty loud. They must like the flower garden. So many places to hide."

"That must be it," Sierra agreed. "Be sure to call me and tell me how everything goes with Nathan. My plane leaves at 10:00 on Wednesday morning. So call me when you get home if it's before 11:00 or else before 9:00 in the morning."

"I will. Thanks for the skirt. See you later."

Amy left in a whirlwind, and Sierra surveyed the rearranged mess in her room.

"I don't want to clean this right now," she muttered.

She flopped onto her bed and listened to the night creatures. Tucking her chin, she lowered her voice to the basement of her range and tried to imitate the croaking frog.

I'll clean my room tomorrow, she decided.

However, Sierra's good intentions didn't work out. Monday night after she finished volunteering at the Highland House, she ended up going with Randy to his band practice. For almost two hours, she sat in a stuffy, closed garage, listening to the four guys work and rework the same song. She couldn't believe she had agreed to come.

When she and Randy finally left, they stopped for something to eat, and by the time she got home, all she wanted to do was crash. Not even the cricket chorus kept her from floating off into dreamland.

Tuesday was just as hectic. She worked at Mama Bear's Bakery in the morning, went to the Highland House from 2:00 to 5:00 and then back to Mama Bear's for two more hours.

Finally, at 8:30 on Tuesday night, Sierra scrambled to throw a bunch of clothes into a travel bag and wrap her gift for Doug and Tracy.

Knowing how much Tracy liked tea, Sierra had found a unique Polish pottery teapot at the Portland Saturday Market a few weeks earlier. She had discovered teacups at another stand that went nicely with the pot, and now she was having a terrible time trying to wrap it all in tissue and find a box big enough for the gift.

By 8:30 the next morning, Sierra had all her things together and was lugging her bag downstairs when Amy called. Mom came into the entryway where Sierra had dumped her bag and handed her the cordless phone.

"Hi," Sierra said. "I was just leaving. I'm glad you caught me. So? Tell me everything really fast. Where did you go? What did you do? Did you have a good time?"

"I can say it all in a few words. I'm in love." Amy sighed on the phone.

Sierra laughed. "Come on. Be serious."

"I'm completely serious. Nathan is perfect for me. First he took me to dinner. It wasn't fancy. Just a '50s hamburger place off Belmont. Really cute. Then we went for a long walk in the park. He held my hand, and it was so romantic!"

"Sounds wonderful," Sierra said.

"Oh, there's more wonderful. We went on the swings at the park, and he pushed me for like half an hour. Then we went on the merry-go-round and down the slide together. I laughed so hard. Oh, and your skirt tore just a teeny, tiny bit. You can hardly see it. I'll fix it."

"How did that happen?" Sierra tried not to sound upset.

"It got caught on the slide. It's not really noticeable. Don't be mad."

"I'm not mad. I was just asking."

"Do you want to hear the rest or not?"

Sierra's mom stepped into the entryway and looked over at Sierra where she was sitting on the bottom step. Mom tapped on her watch and gave Sierra a "let's go" look.

"Yes. Talk fast."

"We drove around and went up to this place where you can see the lights all the way down to the river. It's really beautiful. So peaceful. And then . . . Are you sure you want me to tell you?"

"Of course."

"Well, first he kissed me, then I kissed him, and then we kissed some more and . . ."

"Amy!" Sierra squawked into the phone. "Are you serious? Why did you do that?"

"Relax, Sierra! Man! You scared me. All we did was kiss. There's nothing wrong with that. It was really romantic. He had music on and—" Amy stopped and suddenly changed her tone of voice. "I can't believe you just snapped at me like that. I know this was our first date, but there was absolutely nothing wrong with what we did. I don't appreciate your trying to make it seem like I did something wrong."

"Amy, I didn't mean to sound so harsh. But you guys just met. I think you should take it slower, that's all."

Amy didn't say anything. Sierra could hear her breathing on the other end of the line.

"Look, Amy, I'll call you when I come back Sunday night. Maybe we can get together and talk next Monday. Okay?"

"I don't think there's anything to talk about. I try to tell you about the most romantic night of my life, and you judge me. Why can't you just be happy for me? I didn't expect this kind of reaction from you, Sierra."

Mrs. Jensen picked up Sierra's bag and said in a firm voice, "Sierra, we need to go right now if you're going to make your flight."

Sierra nodded at her mom. "I have to go, Amy. I'll see you in a couple of days. Don't do anything . . ." Sierra wasn't sure how to end that sentence.

"What? Don't do anything you wouldn't do?" Amy added sarcastically. "I'm not a nun, Sierra. But I'm not a sleaze either. So don't try to make me feel like one."

"I wasn't," Sierra said. "I'll call you when I get home. Bye." She pushed the "off" button and stood to take the bag from her mom.

"Everything okay?" her mom asked.

"I guess so. I don't know. Amy met this guy at work, and now suddenly she's in love." They walked down the front porch steps to the van. "Amy's so impulsive. I worry about her sometimes."

"I understand," Mrs. Jensen said, getting into the van and sticking the keys into the ignition. "Do you have your ticket?"

"Yes, in my backpack," Sierra said, pulling her ever faithful companion off her shoulder and unzipping the front pouch. "Right here." She flipped it open and read the printed information. "It leaves at 10:12. We should make it with no problem."

"And you have the gift?"

"In my bag. That's why it's so heavy. I hope it doesn't get thrashed."

Sierra sat back as Mrs. Jensen headed for the freeway that would take them to the Portland airport. Something about the words Sierra just said echoed in the back of her mind. The image of her beautiful wedding gift mangled with the bow squished and the corner torn wouldn't go away. She thought of how embarrassed she would be to hand such a gift to her friends.

Then she thought of Amy. *That's why I reacted so strongly when Amy said she and Nathan had sat in his car and made out,* Sierra realized. Only a few days earlier, Sierra had told her dad she saw herself as a present that she wanted to give to her future husband, and she wanted the wrapping to be perfect.

Maybe what Amy did with Nathan wasn't wrong according to Amy's standards or values. But how could her "wrapping" help but get messed up? Sierra wished she'd had more time to talk with her friend. She and Amy had never discussed their standards before. Maybe Amy didn't have a creed like Sierra did. But would she even be willing to hear Sierra's opinions?

At the departures lane of the airport, Sierra gave her mom a hug good-bye and checked her luggage. Since she had packed in such a hurry, she had taken more clothes than she needed. The thought comforted her, knowing that all the layers of clothing would serve as protective padding for the wedding present.

With her ticket in hand and backpack over her shoulder, Sierra hurried to the gate and arrived just as the passengers began boarding her flight. She got right on, stuffed her backpack under the seat in front of her, and looked out the window.

Sierra decided the first thing she would do when she came back was call Amy. The only problem was that Amy might not want to hear what Sierra had to say.

Chapter Six

STANDING WITH THE REST OF THE TRAVELERS, Sierra waited for the mob to move down the center aisle of the plane and head out the door into the airport. She knew Tawni would be waiting for her. Tawni was meticulous about many things. Being on time to pick up people was one of them.

Sure enough, as Sierra entered the airport, the first person she laid eyes on was her stunning sister. Only, Sierra was startled to see that Tawni had colored her hair. Instead of her natural blond, Tawni's hair was a rich mahogany. The brownish-red color made her look even more sophisticated and grown-up.

During Tawni's months in California, she had landed a job modeling for a small local company. In every way, she looked like a model standing there waiting for Sierra.

"Were you at the back of the plane?" Tawni said, giving Sierra a less than exuberant hug.

"No, the middle."

"Oh. It seemed to take so long for you to get off."

"Can't you say, 'Hi, Sierra! I'm so glad to see you'?

Why do you have to criticize me for taking too long to get off the plane?"

"I wasn't criticizing you. Of course I'm glad to see you."

They walked silently, side by side, to the baggage claim. Finally, Sierra said, "I'm sorry, Tawni. I had some stuff on my mind, I guess. Your hair looks nice. How's everything going?"

"Terrific. I have another offer for a catalog shoot, so that's good. They pay pretty well. At least better than the jobs I've been getting this past month modeling in restaurants."

"Modeling in restaurants?"

"I work for a boutique that's next to a nice restaurant in Carlsbad. Every day for the lunch rush, I walk around the restaurant in different outfits from the boutique. I tell people about what I'm wearing and give out cards from the boutique. The money is okay. It's not many hours, though."

"I've never heard of that kind of modeling."

"It's popular here."

Tawni directed Sierra toward the luggage carousel and continued talking as they waited for Sierra's bag to come rolling by.

"The shoot for the Castle Clothes Catalog will be in La Jolla, which isn't too far from where I live. It's four or five days of work. That should add up to some decent money."

"How's Jeremy?"

"Wonderful," Tawni said, a contented smile curling her lips.

"Did Christy call you? I don't know where I'm staying."

"At Marti's. Christy didn't tell you?"

"You mean at Christy's aunt and uncle's house? Am I the only one staying there?" Sierra asked anxiously. She had been to the luxurious beach house before, and although it was a fantastic place, Sierra wasn't too fond of Christy's Aunt Marti. Tawni was, though, because Marti was the one who had encouraged Tawni to start a modeling career.

"Don't worry. Christy and Katie are staying there, too."

"There's my bag. I'll get it."

Sierra carefully lifted her bag from the conveyor belt and followed Tawni out to the parking lot.

"Are you hungry?" Tawni asked. "Do you want to stop for lunch before I take you over to Bob and Marti's? I took off the afternoon, and they're not expecting you at a specific time anyway."

Sierra noted this friendly gesture on Tawni's part. It wasn't often that Tawni volunteered to spend time socially with Sierra, so Sierra knew she had better take advantage of the offer.

"Sure. Where do you want to go? It'll be my treat. I've been working like crazy all summer, and I have way too much money."

Tawni raised her delicate eyebrows as she unlocked the car door. "Well, then I will let you pay. It'll only be a matter of time, though, before you buy a car or move out. Then see how quickly money evaporates."

They drove down to the beach and found a quiet little café a few blocks from the ocean. It was a garden restaurant, and the entrance was through a white picket gate. Honeysuckle vines laced their long fingers in and out of the garden's latticework and sprinkled their sweet fragrance over Tawni and Sierra as they entered.

"I saw this place a couple of weeks ago and thought it looked fun. I tried to talk Jeremy into taking me here, but he wasn't too thrilled. I guess it's more of a sisters' kind of place."

Tawni's words warmed Sierra. *We really must be growing up,* she thought. Going to lunch together at a garden cottage restaurant was something women, not girls, did with their sisters.

The hostess ushered them to a round patio table under a pale-yellow canvas umbrella and handed them menus printed on long sheets of paper with bright daisy borders. Everything was made fresh that day, according to the menu. The specialty of the house was, of course, garden salads.

For the next two hours, Sierra and Tawni talked and laughed and fully enjoyed each other's company—Sierra loved hearing all about Tawni's relationship with Jeremy. Deep down, she knew it wasn't only because Jeremy was Tawni's devoted boyfriend but also because Jeremy was Paul's brother. Hearing about Jeremy was, in a tiny way, like hearing about Paul.

When the bill came, Sierra was shocked to see that it totaled nearly 30 dollars. She had brought twice that with her, so it wasn't a problem paying. It was just hard to believe that two salads, an appetizer sampler tray, and two raspberry iced teas could add up to that much. She decided this must be the price of passing into womanhood. Times like this with her sister were worth it.

When they got back into Tawni's car, Tawni said, "I noticed your new ring. I was waiting for you to tell me who gave it to you."

"Oh," Sierra said, fingering the gold band with her thumb. "Well, actually . . ." She didn't know if she should tell the whole story about dinner with her dad and the ring he also had for Tawni, or if she should brush it off as nothing important.

"Did it come from a secret admirer?" Tawni asked with a tease in her voice. "Randy maybe?"

"No, it's definitely not from Randy. It's actually from Dad."

"From Dad?"

Sierra nodded.

Tawni pulled her sedan out onto Pacific Coast Highway, her eyes wide with surprise. "Dad gave you a gold ring?"

"It was Wesley's idea to get gold. Dad was going to buy me silver, but I think Wes wanted gold because he got one, too. It's a purity ring. There's a verse engraved inside, and it's a reminder that I've promised God I'll stay pure until marriage."

Tawni didn't say anything.

"Dad bought one for you, too," Sierra said. "I don't know if I was supposed to say anything. He asked if I wanted to bring it with me, and I said I thought he should give it to you. He's going to figure out when he can come down. You could call him and tell him I told you, and he could just send it to you."

"That's okay. It doesn't matter."

Sierra got nervous when her sister said things like that. Tawni was the only one of the six Jensen kids who was adopted. Every now and then it seemed she saw herself as the outsider. Sierra knew it was possible that Tawni would feel that way now about the ring. She wished she would have realized how important it would be to bring the ring with her so she could give it to Tawni.

"A purity ring is a nice symbol for someone your age. I'm glad Dad got it for you."

"I'm sorry, Tawni. I should have brought yours."

"It doesn't matter. Really."

A thick silence enveloped them for a moment.

"I suppose I should tell you the plans, or at least the plans I know about, for the weekend," Tawni said, smoothly changing the subject. "There's a shower scheduled tonight for Tracy at her parents' house, and the guys are having a party for Doug at his parents' house. Tomorrow I have to work, and then I'll be back up Friday afternoon right after work for the wedding, which is here in Newport Beach."

"I just realized," Sierra said, "I don't have a gift for the shower."

"You could split the cost with me on my gift if you want. It could be from both of us."

"That's a great idea. How much do you want for my half?"

"Just 22 dollars."

Twenty-two dollars! I'm going through money like water! Sierra thought.

They pulled into Bob and Marti's driveway. An old VW bus was parked in front of the house, looking out of place in the upscale neighborhood.

"What is that doing here, I wonder?" Sierra thought aloud.

"Didn't you ever see ol' Gus? That's Todd's bus. The last I heard, he was thinking of burying it for good. He must have found another burst of life in the guy."

Tawni set the parking brake and popped open the trunk for Sierra.

When Sierra pulled out her bag and closed the trunk, Tawni was already at the front door, ringing the doorbell. Marti, a petite, well-groomed brunette, answered and greeted Tawni by kissing the air on each side of her cheeks.

When Marti saw Sierra, she graciously extended her manicured hand and said, "So nice to see you again."

Sierra lumbered her way through the front door, trying hard not to bang her luggage on anything. They had barely closed the door behind them when Christy's Uncle Bob came bursting in from the family room and gave each of the girls a hearty hug.

"Welcome, welcome," he said. "Here, let me take that for you."

Sierra found it hard not to stare at him. When she had

first met Uncle Bob over Easter vacation, he had impressed her as an energetic, healthy man. Shorter and stockier than her father, Bob was tan, with thick, dark hair and a friendly twinkle in his eye. He was a good-looking man, not movie star material but definitely attractive. But that Easter break, he had been in a terrible accident when a gas barbecue exploded.

Now Sierra could see the extent of his burns. From his ear, now deformed, down the entire left side of his neck, Bob's skin was red, shriveled, and scarred. Even though Sierra had been there when the accident happened, she had no idea how bad it was.

The trauma had deeply affected Bob. At the end of that week, he announced that he had given his life to Christ. The accident had made him realize how short life was and how he needed to make peace with God. Sierra had left Newport Beach at Easter thinking the accident had had a happy ending.

Now, seeing what Bob had to live with day in and day out for the rest of his life, Sierra wasn't sure the ending was so great. Bob was headed for heaven, but for the rest of his life on earth he would be scarred.

Sierra's thoughts flipped back to Amy. What if she kept going further and further with Nathan? Sierra shivered. *Although something good can come from an "accident,"* Sierra realized, *somebody always ends up scarred for life.*

Chapter Seven

"COME ON IN," BOB SAID TO THE NEW arrivals. "Todd and Christy are out on the patio. Would you like something to drink? How about lunch? Are you hungry?"

"No thanks. We stopped on the way." Tawni checked her watch. "I should get going. I'm supposed to pick up the cake for the shower tonight, and I'm not sure how long it's going to take me to get it and drive to Tracy's."

"Go ahead," Bob said on his way upstairs with Sierra's bag. "Come back whenever you want. We have plans for dinner here, you know. The invitation is open to anyone who wants to come."

"Thanks," Tawni said. She turned to Marti. "If Jeremy calls, would you please let him know where I am? I'll probably be back here at about 5:30. He's coming up with some of the guys from San Diego, but I don't know how late they will arrive."

"I'll tell him," Marti said. "Would you like to take my cell phone with you? That way you can check in if you need to."

"That's okay," Tawni said.

"No, really. I insist." Marti reached for her purse, which sat on a marble-top table by the staircase, and handed Tawni the phone. "Here. You have our number with you, don't you? Call and check in."

"Okay. Thanks. I'll see you later, Sierra." Tawni swished out the door with the cellular phone in her hand, leaving Marti and Sierra alone in the entryway.

Sierra smiled.

Marti smiled back.

It might have been her imagination, but Sierra didn't think Marti liked her much. Sierra felt a little guilty because she didn't particularly care for Marti either.

Marti lifted her chin and said sweetly, "Well, I suppose we should try to find Todd and Christy."

She led Sierra through the elegant living room toward the back patio.

"Oh, Christy," Marti called out before they reached the patio door. "Your friend is here, Christina."

They stepped out onto the patio that faced the glorious beach and deep-blue ocean. Christy and Todd were sitting across from each other under the umbrella of the patio table. They were holding hands and looking intensely at each other.

Sierra felt certain she and Marti had just interrupted a private moment. She wished they hadn't burst onto the patio.

Todd sprang to his feet and gave Sierra a welcoming hug. Christy was right behind him with another big hug. The two friends pulled apart and looked at each other with joyful smiles and excited hellos.

Sierra could tell that, despite the smile, tears were
brimming on Christy's eyelids. She was holding them
back with willpower, but Sierra was sure Christy would
have let them roll down her cheeks if Sierra and Marti
hadn't interrupted them. Sierra knew she wouldn't be at
peace until she had a chance to ask Christy privately if
everything was okay.

"How was your trip down here?" Todd asked. His
warm smile and steady gaze comforted Sierra. Either Todd
wasn't as upset as Christy, or he was much better at
concealing his feelings.

"Fine. It was a smooth trip. Tawni and I stopped for
lunch at a really fun place, which was nice," Sierra replied.

Bob joined them on the patio. Sierra casually gave
Christy another look. She seemed to be swallowing her
tears quickly.

"Your bag is up in the guest room," Bob said. "Now, is
there anything else? Did you want to call home and let
them know you arrived safely? Or don't you jet-set kids
do that kind of thing anymore?"

"I can call later," Sierra said. "Actually, I'll need to call
a friend, too."

"You're welcome to make the calls now," Bob said.

Sierra wondered if Amy would be home. "Then I guess
I'll go ahead and try to call, if that's okay."

"Sure. Help yourself. Nearest phone is in the kitchen."

"Yes, I remember," Sierra said, heading back inside.
The kitchen phone was the one Christy and Sierra had run
to when they called 911 the day of Bob's accident. It felt

strange to retrace those steps now, months later.

Sierra dialed her home number and got their voice mail. She left a quick message letting her parents know she had arrived safely and that everything was fine. She knew her parents would appreciate her checking in.

Then she called Amy. The answering machine picked up Sierra's call, and since she didn't know what kind of message to leave or who might listen to it, she simply said, "Amy, it's Sierra. I'll try to call you later. Bye."

What a wimp! You could have left some kind of coded message like, "Don't forget what I said this morning." Right. Like that's going to change anything. She thinks she's in love with this guy. They're probably together right now.

For a few minutes, Sierra stood silently in the kitchen.

Why am I letting this get to me? Amy is responsible for her own actions. I'm not her guardian angel or her conscience. Still, she becomes serious about guys so fast. What if it's the same way with Nathan? A lot could happen while I'm gone.

"Father God," Sierra prayed in barely a whisper, "I don't know how to pray for Amy. Would You please protect her? Don't let anything bad happen between her and Nathan, please. I really want her to be strong in You and to stay pure."

Sierra mouthed an "Amen" to close her prayer and headed back to join the others. But nothing inside her felt comforted. How could she be peaceful when her closest friend at home was in over her head with some guy, and when her dear friend Christy was nearly in tears?

Relationships! Why do I think I'll be able to figure out my own with a simple list and a creed? I can't even cope when my friends are involved in intense relationships.

Sierra stopped in the middle of the living room and realized her thinking was wrong. She wasn't in charge of her friends' lives or their relationships. All she needed to concentrate on was her most important relationship, the one with the Lord.

A not-so-favorite feeling stirred in Sierra's stomach. Whenever she had these little glimmers of insight, it usually meant God was about to teach her something. And that meant she was going to be stretched. She didn't like this part of growing up.

Sierra slipped quietly out onto the patio. Bob was standing by the low brick wall, talking to a neighbor. The older, nearly bald man had been walking his little terrier on a retractable leash. Marti sat with Todd and Christy at the table under the shady umbrella; she was talking animatedly and had the couple's attention.

Not quite sure where she fit in, Sierra walked over to the wall and held out her hand to the small dog. It yipped loudly, and its owner pulled on the leash.

"Sorry," Sierra said sheepishly.

"Nothing to be sorry about," the man said. "You hush, Mittsey."

Christy came up next to Sierra and said, "Do you feel like going for a walk?"

"Sure."

"We'll be back in about an hour," Christy said to her uncle.

"Okey dokey."

Sierra noticed as they stepped over the brick wall that Marti was still talking at full speed to Todd, but his eyes followed Christy as they left.

"Do you mind walking in the sand?" Christy asked.

"No. I love it. I'm glad you suggested this."

"And I'm glad you're here," Christy said. She pulled a ponytail holder from her wrist and gathered her nutmeg-brown hair into a high ponytail. Christy was taller than Sierra and moved through the sand with what Sierra considered a casual gracefulness.

Christy wasn't elegant like Tawni. And she wasn't particularly beautiful. But what made Christy striking was her open face and clear-eyed honesty. She had distinctive blue-green eyes, which were once again filling with tears.

"So much has happened in the last few days," Christy said as she directed Sierra toward the shore, where they could walk more easily in the firmly packed sand. "I feel as if my head is so full of information that it's going to crash like a computer hard drive."

"What's going on?" Sierra slipped off her sandals and let her toes mesh into the hot sand.

Dozens of beachgoers were scattered along the shoreline. Little kids played in the water, laughing and squealing. The carefree scene around them was a stark contrast to the downcast mood that hung over Christy.

She let out a long, deep breath. "I just found out I've

been accepted at the school I wanted to attend. They turned me down last spring; so I went on with other plans. Now they have an opening, and I have two weeks to decide if I'm going."

The curling hand of an ocean wave unfurled at their feet, shocking Sierra's toes with its cold fingers.

"And you're having a hard time deciding if you still want to go?"

Christy nodded.

They walked quietly for a few minutes, letting the playful Pacific grab their ankles and then run away. Sierra glanced at Christy and saw the first tear break over the rim of her lower lid and slide down her cheek.

"The school is in Switzerland," Christy said softly.

Chapter Eight

*S*IERRA WALKED ALONGSIDE CHRISTY IN SILENCE. Sierra knew such a decision would be hard for Christy. What would happen to Todd and Christy's relationship if she were far away? Would it be jeopardized by the distance between them? Then there was the adventure factor. The two friends had talked about this on the phone. They had decided that the trip to England, when they had met the previous January, had been more to Sierra's liking than to Christy's. Even though Christy said she liked the trip and wouldn't change any of the things God did, by nature she was more of a homebody.

"I can see how this would be a hard decision for you," Sierra said.

"It shouldn't be, I suppose," Christy said, sounding irritated with herself. "I mean, who wouldn't want to go to Switzerland? It's a unique program that gives me college units along with work-experience credits, so it would be almost like two years of study in one."

"You would be gone for a year?"

"Yes," Christy said, her voice growing dim. "It's a minimum commitment of six months, but they really want you to stay a year. The work experience is at an orphanage, and it's too hard on the children if the workers leave every few months."

As they walked on, Christy explained more about the program. She knew it would prepare her for what she wanted to do—to work with small children in a ministry setting. "But it means I'll be leaving Todd and my family for all that time, and I don't know if I want to do that."

"What do your parents think?" Sierra asked.

"They think it's a wonderful opportunity and that it's up to me to decide. I've been offered a scholarship. My parents could never afford to put me through a program like this. They said they'll support whatever I choose to do. They're praying I'll make the right decision."

"And Todd?" Sierra ventured.

Another tear skittered down Christy's cheek. "He's praying I'll make the right decision, too."

Sierra tried to imagine what it would feel like to make such a gigantic decision. She knew if it were her choice, she would fly off to Switzerland in a second. But if a guy like Todd were in her life, she knew it would be much more complicated. Her next question was simplistic, but she had to ask it.

"Could Todd go to Switzerland, too?"

"Not really. He's taken his college courses in too many pieces. He's been to three universities and then worked on a correspondence course while he was in Spain. He needs almost a full year of courses before he can get his B.A. There's nothing in Switzerland that we know of that would provide that for him." Christy stopped walking and let out a sigh. "Do you mind if we sit for a while?"

"Not at all."

They trudged through the sand to an open spot away from the summer crowds and sat down.

"Man, this sand is hot!" Sierra said.

"Try scooping off the top layer," Christy said, demonstrating. "That's what Todd does. Either that or he turns his thongs upside down and sits on the bottoms of them."

Sierra tried to scoop the hot sand away and settled back down. "Much better," she said. "But I felt like a cat digging in its litter box."

Christy laughed. It seemed to break the tension.

"So, tell me what's been happening with you," Christy said. "I've been giving you all my problems, and I haven't even asked how you're doing."

"There's not much to tell," Sierra said with a wink. "I'm not being offered scholarships to schools in Switzerland."

"Yet," Christy said with a smile. "Your chance will come soon enough."

"And you will have gone through it all and have made all the right decisions," Sierra teased. "So when it's my turn, you can tell me what to do."

Christy laughed again. "Don't count on it! If there's one thing I've learned, it's that God is a very creative author, and He writes a different story for every person. No two lives or stories are alike."

"Next thing you're going to tell me is there's not another Todd floating around in this world just waiting to meet someone like me."

A tender smile curled Christy's lips. Then she pursed them together in a tight, contemplative expression. "You know," she said slowly, "everyone thinks Todd is the perfect guy."

"And you don't?"

"He's not perfect," Christy said. "He's an only child, and his parents are divorced. So sometimes it's hard for him to connect and be open with people."

"But he's close to you, isn't he? And your family?"

"Yes. I guess what I'm trying to say is that this decision about Switzerland is really hard for me, and I don't think he completely understands because he's done so much moving around. He would have no problem picking up and leaving for a year. He's done that before. To me it's an overwhelming decision."

"May I ask you something kind of personal?" Sierra asked.

"Sure."

"Are you afraid your relationship will fall apart if you go away to school?"

"I don't know. I think it would last. We've been through a lot already. But then, a year is a really long time. People change."

"Did you change when Todd went to Spain?"

"Yes, I suppose I did."

"But you were still right for each other when you met up again."

"Yes."

"This might be naive," Sierra said, shifting her position in the sand, "but what's one more test of your relationship after all you've been through? I mean, true love waits, right?"

Christy swallowed hard and nodded. "Yes, true love waits," she repeated. "But don't ever let anyone tell you it's an easy thing to do."

Sierra looked over at Christy, smiled, and said with confidence, "I think you should go to Switzerland, and you and Todd should write letters to each other every week. It would be the ultimate endless romance. Then one day when you're sitting in your rocking chairs and all your teeth have fallen out, you can show those letters to your great-grandchildren, and they'll have them bronzed or something."

Christy burst out laughing. "You really have a way of putting things into a different perspective, Sierra."

Sierra laughed with her. "Think about it," she said more seriously. "You have the rest of your life to be with Todd if he really is the right guy for you, which none of the rest of us seems to doubt. But you might not always have the chance to go to Switzerland."

"I know, you're right," Christy said.

"Not that it makes it any easier to take off for a whole year, and not that I have any idea how hard it would be or how much you would miss Todd. But think of it, Christy—Switzerland!"

Sierra did her best to imitate a carefree yodel, which made Christy laugh.

"There's only one flaw in your romantic scheme," Christy said.

"What's that?"

"In all the years I've known Todd, I've never gotten a single letter from him."

"Then I'd say it's about time he started writing!" Sierra said. She felt a little pang in her heart after she spoke. Paul had written to her months ago, and her response had been flippant. What did she know about starting up a romantic correspondence? Who was she to give advice to Christy and Todd?

"You know what?" Sierra said. "You shouldn't listen to me. I think you should pray, and I'll pray, too, and whatever God directs you to do, that's what you should do."

Christy nodded. "This is my story, I guess, isn't it? I have no clue what will happen in the next chapter of my life. All I know is that I want God to be free to write with His pen. Do you feel like praying with me now?"

"Of course. Sure."

Under the deep-blue August sky, Sierra and Christy bowed their heads together and asked the Lord, the Author and Finisher of their faith, to write the next chapter of both their lives with His grace and majesty.

Then, done praying and ready to face the others, they sauntered through the sand back to Bob and Marti's house.

"I'm so glad you came," Christy said. "I feel lighter somehow. I still don't know what I'm going to do, but I feel a lot better about everything. I know everything will work out. It always does."

Sierra thought of Amy. *Will everything turn out okay for her? Or does it only turn out okay for those who diligently seek God in every area of their lives?* Sierra knew Amy wasn't doing that, though. How could she be seeking God if it was so easy for her to physically express herself with a guy she barely knew?

Amy was settling for less than God's best. That's what Sierra would tell her. And Amy would see Sierra's point, and once she did, she was sure to change her opinion about Nathan.

Chapter Nine

SIERRA TRIED TO CALL AMY AFTER SIERRA AND Christy arrived back at the house. This time Sierra left a message on the answering machine. "Hi, Aim. I've been thinking about our talk this morning, and I'm still positive I'm right. I just wanted to encourage you to never settle for anything less than God's best. You know what I mean. I'll talk to you when I get home. See you."

She hung up with a sense of accomplishment. *Now I can concentrate on my friends here.*

Just then the doorbell rang. From the sounds that echoed from the direction of the open door, Sierra knew Katie had arrived. Katie Weldon, an exuberant redhead with a quick wit, was already teasing Uncle Bob.

"Be careful with that bag, mister. My only nice clothes in the world are in there, and they're already ironed. Better keep that in mind or there won't be a tip for you."

Sierra stepped into the entryway, and Katie's mischievous green eyes flashed in her direction.

"Sierra!" she screamed. "When did you get here?" She rushed to tackle Sierra in a hug.

"A few hours ago," Sierra answered, her face crushed against Katie's shoulder.

The only one who gave wilder hugs than Katie was Doug. Sierra had a feeling she was going to get her fill of hugs from all her buddies this week.

"All right! Let the fun begin!" Katie said, looking over her shoulder at Todd, Christy, and Marti. "Who else is here?"

"This is it," Todd said. "The other guys are over at Doug's. You know about the shower tonight for Tracy, don't you?"

"Yep. Got my present in my bag. Hey," she called up the stairs, "be extra careful with that bag, mister. Valuable gifts are inside."

Bob appeared at the top of the stairs and played along with the bellboy role. "Would you like me to hang your garments for you, miss?"

"No thanks. You can tell me how to order room service, though. I'm starved."

"Aren't you always?" Marti said under her breath.

Sierra guessed she was the only one who heard it. She wondered how long Marti had been carrying on this love-hate relationship with Christy's friends. Katie was certainly not one of Marti's favorites, like Tawni was. In a way, Sierra felt glad for her sister. In their large family, Tawni had never been anyone's pet. Sierra always felt Granna Mae paid more attention to her than to Tawni. Maybe this made a good balance. Finally, Tawni had someone to dote on her.

"The lasagna should be out of the oven in five minutes," Bob said, checking his watch as he came down the stairs. "Anyone want to help me throw together a salad?"

They all agreed to help and made their way into the kitchen while Katie chattered nonstop. Sierra was given the task of setting the table. Todd went to work with Christy tossing the salad in a big wooden bowl, but Bob kept finding new items in the refrigerator to add to the mix. Marti slipped out. Katie talked about her new job at a coffee bar inside an upscale bookstore.

"If you guys want, I can whip up some killer cappuccinos for dessert. You still have that espresso machine around here, don't you?"

"It's in the cupboard above the oven," Bob said. He pulled cans of soda from the pantry and filled glasses with ice. "Cappuccinos sure sound good to me. I'd better get this garlic bread in the oven. Could you help me, Sierra?"

Sierra took the long loaf of sourdough garlic bread from Bob and wrapped it loosely in foil. As she opened the oven door to slide in the bread, the whole kitchen filled with the mouth-watering aroma of lasagna. The tomato sauce along the edges of the huge pan bubbled over the sides.

"Man, that smells good," Todd said. He popped open a can of soda and leaned in to have a look at their dinner. "Did you make that, Bob?"

"Sure did."

"You'll have to teach Todd your secret recipe for

tomato sauce, Uncle Bob," Christy said. "He made some spaghetti last week at his dad's and it was, well . . ." Christy gave Todd a tender look and didn't finish her sentence.

"It was out of a can," Todd said, unaffected by Christy's gentle criticism. "The only kind I know how to make."

"It's all in the spices," Bob said.

The doorbell rang again. A minute later, Tawni and Jeremy entered the kitchen. Broad-shouldered, dark-haired Jeremy had a wide grin on his face and his arm around Tawni's shoulder. They looked good together, even though Sierra was having a hard time adjusting to Tawni's mahogany-colored hair.

"Smells like we came to the right place," Jeremy said. "Hi, Sierra. How're you doing?" He came over and gave her a sideways hug. "Tawni said you had a good trip down. It's nice to see you."

"It's nice to see you, too."

Jeremy greeted the rest of them. Bob pulled out two more plates and added them to the stack at the end of the buffet serving line he had set up on the counter.

"Any of the other guys coming?" Bob asked.

"I think they're all eating at Doug's," Jeremy said. "Tawni said you had enough for one more person."

"There's always enough," Bob said. "And you're always welcome. Where's my wife? We're about ready to eat. Todd, why don't you pull out the lasagna and let it cool a few minutes? I'll go find Marti."

Todd obliged and placed the heavy pan on top of the

stove. Sierra retrieved the warmed bread, and Christy turned off the oven. They lined up, ready to dig in.

"She'll be here in a minute. She's on the phone," Bob said, stepping back into the kitchen. "Shall we pray?"

Todd reached for Christy's hand and bowed his head. Jeremy took Tawni's hand.

"Why don't we all hold hands?" Bob asked. "I like it when we do that."

He reached for Sierra's left hand and Christy took her right. Then Bob prayed the most unique prayer Sierra had ever heard.

"Will You just look at us here, God? You did all this. You brought us all together again, and I'm grateful to You for it. We have some food here, which, of course, You provided out of Your bountiful goodness to us. We appreciate that, too. Now we want to ask for something. Will You let Your kingdom come and Your will be done on earth as it's all planned out in heaven? That would be great. I'm asking this in the name of Christ Jesus."

Sierra kept her eyes closed, waiting for an "Amen." There wasn't one. Everyone let go of hands and began to talk at once. A sweet closeness enfolded the group.

Sierra felt close to Randy, Amy, and her other friends from school, but it wasn't the same as this. Sierra's relationships here somehow felt clearer and less complicated.

"It's so gooey!" Katie said as Todd tried to serve her a slab of the steaming lasagna.

"The only kind of lasagna worth eating is gooey

lasagna," Jeremy said. "Better get your plate in here, Sierra, before Todd. I've seen that guy eat more than any human being should."

"Except Doug," Katie corrected him. "Nobody eats as much as Doug."

"Yeah, good ol' Doug," Todd said, giving Jeremy a mischievous look. "I wonder how the ol' bachelor is doing about now?"

"He's fine now," Jeremy said. "Try asking that question again around midnight."

The two guys exchanged knowing glances and chuckled. Sierra had no idea why Doug should be any different at midnight than he was right now. The wedding wasn't until Friday, two days away.

"Wonderful news!" Marti said, bursting into the kitchen and waving some papers above her head. "They're still valid. I made the reservations for Sunday. It's all set!"

Everyone looked at Marti, then at each other, and finally at Bob for an explanation. Bob shook his head. He was as much in the dark about Marti's exciting news as they were.

"What's all set?" Christy asked.

"Switzerland!" Marti announced. "We're going to Switzerland!"

"Who's going to Switzerland?" Christy asked cautiously.

"Why, you, Todd, and me, of course."

Todd looked the most surprised of all. "What? When are we going?"

"Sunday. Weren't you listening?"

"This Sunday?" Todd and Christy said in unison.

"Yes, this Sunday! I'm cashing in our last three vouchers, and the travel agent is making the hotel reservations right now. Don't look so shocked. We'll only be gone for a week."

Todd looked at Christy and then back at Marti. "There's one minor problem," he said.

"What's that?" Marti asked.

Todd stuck the spatula back into the lasagna and, without looking up, said calmly, "I can't go."

Chapter Ten

"DON'T BE ABSURD," MARTI SAID. "OF course you can go! I've planned this whole trip so Christy can see the school and the orphanage. The least you can do, Todd Spencer, is show some support for Christy and come along so you can help her make this important decision."

Todd looked at Marti. It seemed to Sierra that his chin stuck out in a gesture of resolution. "Christy is capable of making decisions without my telling her what to do. God is the One who will help her make this choice, not me. I can't take the time off from work. I've already used up the last of my time off for Doug's wedding."

Marti looked stumped. "This is not what I expected you to say, Todd."

"I'll go!" Katie volunteered.

"Fine." Marti slapped the three airline vouchers on the counter and dramatically held up her hands in surrender. "They're all yours, Christina. Three seats on Sunday morning's flight to Switzerland. Do with them as you will. You probably don't even want me to go. That's fine. It's my gift to you." Marti's voice toned down a notch and some of the edge softened. "I know this has been a difficult decision for you. I remembered we had these free flight credits, so I thought it might help if you could see what the school was like. Then you would know if you wanted to go or not."

Christy put down her plate and stepped over to her aunt. Giving Marti a warm hug, Christy added a quick kiss on the cheek. Sierra had to admire Christy. It seemed more appropriate to shake the woman rather than hug her. Why hadn't Marti asked anyone before plunging forward with her grand plan? And what about Bob? Why didn't she plan for him to go on the trip?

"I really appreciate it, Aunt Marti," Christy said. "I know you meant well. But I don't need to go. It's okay. You can use these for another trip for you and Uncle Bob."

"No, I can't." Marti sniffed and looked at Todd. "I've already transferred them to the Sunday flight. I won't change my plans. You have no reason you can't go next week, Christina. So there are the three tickets. One for you and two for whomever you wish to invite. You don't have to include me in the trip if you don't want."

"You know what?" Christy said. "I'd like to have some time to think about all this. Would it be okay if I let you know a little later?"

Marti slowly picked up the vouchers. "I suppose. Let me know what you decide. The sooner the better."

"Okay. Thanks, Aunt Marti. I really appreciate it."

The crowd quietly carried their plates over to the kitchen table. Once they were seated, the noise level began to increase. Sierra sat next to Tawni and noticed Marti had left the kitchen, still wearing a hurt expression. In Sierra's opinion, Christy deserved a medal for the way she handled the awkward situation. Sierra was certain she wouldn't have been so gracious.

They talked and ate for almost an hour. First they consumed the lasagna, garlic bread, and salad. Then they indulged in Katie's expertly prepared coffee beverages. The evening continued at a leisurely pace until Tawni noticed the time and suggested they leave for Tracy's shower.

Bob went to see if Marti was ready to go. Katie ran upstairs for her gift. Christy stepped into the family room to talk privately with Todd, and Tawni slipped out to use the rest room. Jeremy and Sierra were left alone to clear the table.

"How has your summer been?" Jeremy asked.

"It's gone fast," Sierra said.

"I hear from my uncle that you've been doing amazing things with the kids at the Highland House. They sure are glad you've helped out."

"I really enjoy it," Sierra said. "The kids seem to appreciate everything I do with them. Two weeks ago, a couple of the younger girls asked when I was going to tell them some more Bible stories. That was definitely a change from when I first went there."

"Paul told me your first few Bible story attempts didn't go over so well."

The minute Sierra heard Jeremy mention Paul's name, her heart began to beat wildly. She had wanted to ask about Paul earlier but hadn't. She was surprised, though, at the way her heart pounded at the mere mention of his name.

"I guess so. I mean, he's right, they didn't." Sierra paused and swallowed hard as she lowered a stack of dishes into the sink. "H-how is your brother?"

Since when did I start stuttering? And why did I say "your brother"? Is it so hard for me to use Paul's name? What's wrong with me?

"My brother is doing extremely well, thanks. He'll be glad to hear you're doing well."

Sierra could feel Jeremy's gaze on her. Was he trying to see if she was blushing? She kept her head down so he couldn't see her face. She remembered how Jeremy and Tawni had rigged up a meeting between Paul and Sierra a few months ago, before he left for Scotland. That night, Paul had made it clear that he wasn't interested in Sierra. Why was Jeremy looking for anything more from her? So he could tease her? *I won't give him the satisfaction,* Sierra decided.

Lifting her head and shaking back her wild, blond curls, Sierra faced Jeremy and said, "And how about you? Have you had a good summer?"

Jeremy hesitated slightly before heading back to the table to clear off the rest of the dishes. "It's been great having Tawni down here. Did she tell you about the sailboat my friend bought? We've been out on it a couple of times. Tawni and I both really love sailing."

"Sounds fun," Sierra said.

Bob entered the kitchen and said, "Thanks, Sierra. I can take it from here. You'd better join the other women. I think they're all ready to go."

"Thanks for a great dinner." Sierra smiled at Bob and imagined that her smile showered him with encouragement. Encouragement was probably something this man didn't receive a lot from his wife.

"Have a wonderful time," Bob called after her as Sierra hurried to join the others.

"Do you have the present?" Sierra asked Tawni.

"Yes, it's in the car. Let's have everyone go in my car since parking might be a problem."

"I don't think we'll all fit," Marti said. She had changed into a pair of wide-legged pants with a long, kaleidoscope-colored silk jacket. It appeared she had bounced back from the rift with Christy and was ready to be in control of something new. "Let's all go in my car. It's bigger."

No one argued. Tawni grabbed the gift from her car and joined them. She slid across the leather backseat of Marti's new Lexus and balanced the large gift box on her lap.

"What did we get her?" Sierra asked.

Tawni gave a feathery laugh. "Oh, you'll see."

Sierra wasn't in the mood to play one of her sister's guessing games, so she let it go. They drove the few short blocks to Tracy's house. Marti slowly edged her car into the driveway and set the parking brake.

Inside Tracy's parents' house, half a dozen women had already gathered. Light instrumental music played in the background. Sierra realized she was underdressed when she noticed the dining room table. On top of the lace tablecloth sat a silver tea service and china teacups. In the middle of the table, candles, flowers, silverware, and china cake plates surrounded the cake Tawni had brought earlier. It was white with light-blue rippled frosting along the sides and was trimmed with real flowers.

Next to the table stood Tracy's mom wearing a flowing summer dress. Sierra glanced down at her shorts and T-shirt. Even Katie had put a blazer on over her cotton shirt, and although she had pushed up the sleeves, the look was dressy. Sierra felt like a tomboy who had dropped out of her tree house into the neighbor's yard and landed in the middle of a proper tea party.

Slipping away from all the visiting women, Sierra found the bathroom down the hallway. She took one look in the mirror and groaned.

"You have to grow up sometime, girl," she scolded herself. "Next time you're invited to a bridal shower, you could at least try brushing your hair before you go."

Using her fingers to untangle some of the wind-whipped snarls, Sierra tried to smooth her hair. She washed her face and brushed her teeth with her finger. Then, shaking out her large T-shirt in an effort to scare away some of the wrinkles, Sierra looked at her reflection.

"Why can't you be like the others?" she muttered to herself. She didn't like this uncomfortable feeling.

What is my style? My image? she thought. *At the dinner with Dad last week, I was uncomfortable being dressed up. Now I'm out of place because I feel underdressed. Where's the middle ground? Who am I trying to be?*

As she joined the party, which had now swelled to nearly 25 women, Sierra told herself she was just being Sierra, and that was fine. She didn't need to change inside, nor did she need to change her outfit.

But then she saw Tracy, the star of the event. Tracy's heart-shaped face absolutely glowed. She wore a cotton sundress and a gold cross on a necklace; her hair was cut shorter than Sierra had ever seen it. She looked older than Sierra remembered from their time together in England. Was it her hair? Or the knowledge that, in two days, she was going to become a married woman? Sierra felt her own confidence shatter. She would have been better off staying in her tree house.

"There you are!" Tracy said as she came over to greet Sierra. "I'm so glad you came. I really appreciate it. Would you like some tea? I know the weather is kind of hot for tea, but I wanted to use my new silver teapot. Did you see it? It was my grandmother's. She gave it to us as a wedding gift. Come over and meet my grandmother."

Sierra knew that Tracy was the kind of friend who looked at the inside. The shorts and T-shirt didn't faze her a bit. That knowledge helped Sierra to hush the condemning inner voices that called her "unrefined" and "immature."

While meeting Tracy's relatives, neighbors, and women from her church, Sierra found out this was Tracy's third shower. Many of the women here were ones who hadn't been able to make it to either of the other two showers. She accepted a cup of tea from Tracy's grandmother, who poured it with her wobbly hand. Thanking her, Sierra found a place to sit down.

She carefully balanced the delicate china cup on the saucer and looked around the room. Everyone was so excited for Tracy.

And they should be, Sierra thought, sipping her tea. *Tracy held out for a hero and look who God gave her.*

The tea immediately warmed Sierra inside. Or was it the cozy, peaceful sensation that came from watching Tracy, her family, and her friends celebrate? The thought helped to redirect Sierra's feelings of insecurity.

This is how I want it to be when I get married. Granna Mae pouring the tea, all my friends laughing and hugging me. And I want to look just like Tracy. She's so beautiful!

Sierra glanced down at the fine china teacup and noticed that the gold band on her finger caught the glow of the candlelight from the end table next to her. It was a strong contrast to the silver bracelets on her arm. That was exactly how she felt in this room—like the silver among the gold.

Chapter Eleven

THE GIFT-OPENING PORTION OF THE SHOWER was in full swing when Tracy lifted a small card from its envelope and announced, "This gift is from Tawni and Sierra." She carefully pulled off the thick white ribbon and handed it to Christy, who was sitting next to her busily making a bouquet from a paper plate and the ribbons taken from Tracy's gifts.

"Almost broke that one," Katie teased. She had announced earlier that every ribbon the bride broke represented a baby she would have. Katie predicted that Tracy would break nine ribbons.

"I did not." Tracy slipped her long thumbnail under the wrapping paper and smiled at her mom.

Sierra mouthed the words, "What is it?" to her sister across the room. Tawni only smiled and nodded toward Tracy, indicating Sierra should watch and see. The gift box bore the name of the boutique Tawni modeled for in Carlsbad. Sierra guessed her sister had received a discount on whatever it was. *And it had better be good for the 22 dollars I contributed,* she thought.

Tracy opened the gift box, laid back the tissue, and expressed surprise and delight. Her cheeks began to turn pink.

"This is beautiful!" she exclaimed, lifting the sheer white fabric carefully from the box for everyone to see.

A chorus of oh's and ah's reverberated around the room. Tracy held up a floor-length white gossamer gown. A string of white ribbons and tiny pearls lined the front.

"That's the robe," Tawni said. She pointed at the box. "There's more."

Tracy lifted the robe all the way out and handed it to her cousin, who sat on the other side of her, listing all the gifts as Tracy opened them. Then she drew from the box a short, sheer nightgown with thin straps.

"This is so pretty!" Tracy said. She held the elegant yet very revealing nightgown in front of her. Every woman in the room had something to say.

Sierra pursed her lips together and glanced around at the delighted guests. Tawni looked pleased that Tracy liked her selection, smiling as if she wouldn't mind having such an outfit for her honeymoon. Christy was feeling the fine white fabric and smiling at Tracy. Tracy's mom admired the nightgown and whispered to Tracy's grandmother that it was a special gift.

"Doesn't leave much to the imagination," Katie quipped.

The women chuckled softly.

Tracy glowed. She shot her mom an excited grin and then carefully folded the gown and robe and tucked them back in the box.

"Thanks so much!" Tracy said, catching Tawni's eye and then looking over at Sierra. "I love it, and I think Doug will, too."

All the women chuckled again. One said, "Oh, you can be sure of that!"

Sierra felt like crying. She was surprised at her reaction. At first, she was embarrassed and a little annoyed at her sister for buying such a revealing outfit and for not telling her ahead of time what it was. Now she felt like crying. It was an emotional experience to watch her friend become excited about her honeymoon and shamelessly show how much she was looking forward to giving her body to her husband for the first time.

Swallowing quickly, Sierra held back the glistening tears that had risen to her eyes. She decided this was a powerful celebration for all these women partly because of Doug and Tracy's purity. They hadn't even kissed yet. Doug had vowed he wouldn't kiss a girl until they were standing at the altar on their wedding day, and he had kept that vow. In two days, he would stand before God and many witnesses and promise himself for life to this special woman. Then he would seal that promise with their very first kiss.

The tears welled up in Sierra's eyes again. She had never kissed a guy, and at this moment, she was intensely glad about that. She didn't know if she wanted to wait until her wedding day for her first kiss, but she knew that when she did kiss a guy, it would mean a lot. A lot more than a first-date experiment, as it seemed to have been for Amy and Nathan.

Tracy held up a bottle of bath oil and lotion from the box on her lap. "Thanks, Heather," she said. "You remembered." She sniffed the top of the bottle. "I love this fragrance."

"There's another box there, too. It has the same wrapping. It's for Doug, but you can open it," Heather said.

Tracy tugged at the ribbon, and it snapped in her hand.

"Aha!" Katie's short red hair swished as she announced, "That's one! And on Doug's present, too. Must mean your first child will be a boy."

Tracy handed Christy the broken ribbon and gave a cute little shrug. She opened the box and started to laugh. "Oh, he'll love this."

"I thought we shouldn't leave Doug out of all the bath-time fun," Heather said.

Tracy lifted out a big bottle of Mr. Sudsy bubble bath.

"That's perfect!" Katie said. "Now you have to name your first child Mr. Sudsy."

Everyone laughed, and Tracy passed the box around the circle.

Forty-five minutes later, Tracy finished opening the gifts. All of them were personal items for her. She received four other nighties, including a long, black one from Aunt Marti. The only duplicate gifts were lotion, but Tracy insisted she would use them both.

The gifts made the rounds of the women sitting in the big circle. Soft music played in the background, and candles gave off a faint scent of lilies.

"Before we cut the cake," said Tracy's mom, standing

and trying to get everyone's attention, "I'd like to say a few things."

Sierra noticed Tracy's mom had a note card in her hand, which was trembling slightly. It reminded Sierra of her dad at the restaurant. Why was it so hard for parents to speak to their children about the things deepest in their hearts?

"When Tracy was born, she weighed only four pounds and two ounces. We had to leave her in the hospital for almost three weeks because her lungs weren't fully developed. I remember sitting by her in the hospital one night, wishing I could take her out of that incubator and hold her in my arms."

The room had grown still as each woman listened. Looks of tender compassion brushed across their faces.

"I remember the day the doctor told me I could take you home," Tracy's mom said, looking over at her daughter. "I thought, 'This is it! This is what I've been waiting for. Now I'm never going to let her go.' Well, that was more than 20 years ago. And now I have to let go."

Women all around the room began to blink. A few reached into their purses for tissues.

"I wanted to say something to you tonight that would let you know how much I love you. I found this poem, and it expresses exactly how I feel. It's called, 'What a Mother Thinks.'"

Tracy's mom cleared her throat and read from her card.

"'I love you so much. / There is no way I can possibly put into words how proud I am of you. / You're absolutely beautiful. / Sometimes when our eyes meet, it's like gazing into a reflecting pool. I see in you glimmers of my past. / Do you see in me hints of your future? / You are everything I ever prayed for. / There's nothing about you I'd change. / I love you more than you will ever know, more than you will ever ask. / There's nothing I wouldn't give for you, nothing I wouldn't do for you. / You are my daughter, and I will always love you with a love so immense, so eternal, I could never find a way to squeeze it into words.'"

Sierra swallowed hard and looked around the room. Everyone was crying.

"Would you please stand, honey? I'd like to bless you."

Tracy stood, and her mother stepped over beside her. They were about the same height. With her short hair, Tracy closely resembled her mom.

Her mother placed her still-quivering hand on Tracy's forehead, and paraphrasing Numbers 6, she said, "May the Lord bless you and keep you, Tracy Lynn. May the Lord make His face shine upon you, and be gracious to you. May the Lord lift up His countenance upon you and give you peace."

The two women looked into each other's eyes and exchanged unspoken words in the way only a mother and daughter can. Then her mom leaned over and, with a kiss on the cheek, whispered something in Tracy's ear that made her smile.

The phone rang, and Katie jumped up to answer it.

"I'd like to first get a picture of Tracy cutting the cake," her mom said. "Then please come help yourselves."

Tracy had positioned herself at the table with the silver cake slicer when Katie burst into the room and said, "Trace, you have to take this call."

"Just a minute," her mother said. "Picture first!"

Tracy smiled, her mom took the shot, and Katie called out, "Hurry up! You have to hear this."

Sierra watched as Tracy took the phone and covered her open ear with her hand. "Hello? . . . Yes . . . Yes . . . No . . . Where? . . . Wait. Who is this? . . . Hello?"

She handed the phone back to Katie. All the younger women had gathered around her.

"What was that all about?" Heather asked.

Tracy closed her eyes and shook her head. "I knew this was going to happen."

"What?"

Tracy let out a deep breath and said, "Anyone want to go with me? The guys have kidnapped Doug. They said they won't let him go unless I come see him first."

"Where is he?" Tracy's mom asked, stepping into the circle.

"They chained him to the Balboa Island Ferry and paid the captain to let him ride all night," Tracy said.

"That doesn't sound so bad," Christy said. "I thought the guys were going to do something really wild."

"You haven't heard the worst," Tracy said. "They said I won't recognize him."

"Why?"

"I think they dressed him in some kind of costume."

"Jeremy wouldn't do anything like that to Doug," Tawni said.

"Guess again," Katie said. "I think that was Jeremy on the phone."

"What kind of costume could he be wearing?" Sierra asked.

Tracy looked around at her friends. "There's only one way to find out. Mom?"

"Go, honey. It's okay. Here! Take the camera. We'll save some cake for you."

Chapter Twelve

SIERRA SQUEEZED INTO THE BACKSEAT OF TRACY'S car along with Christy and Tawni. Katie and another girl were in the front seat and five more followed in Heather's car. Everyone in Tracy's car was talking at once, and the dignity of the earlier hour had vanished.

"I'm going to park on the Newport Beach side," Tracy said. "Let's all walk onto the ferry together. Watch out for these guys. I wouldn't be surprised if they had water balloons ready to launch at us."

"Do you think it's a trick?" Tawni asked.

"Could be," Katie agreed. "They could be setting us up. Maybe they didn't do anything to Doug, and they're just trying to get you to fall into their trap. Did you ever think of that, Trace?"

Tracy stopped the car at a red light and looked over at Katie. "No—think about it. These guys have far more reasons to pull a prank on Doug than they do on me. I kind of wished we had changed clothes, though."

"There wasn't time," Katie said. "Your true love is in

desperate need of your assistance. How can you think of changing into the appropriate attire for a rescue?"

"I like this dress. I want to take it on our honeymoon, and I don't want those baboons to ruin it."

"Hey, that's my baboon you're talking about," Christy said.

"And mine," Tawni added.

"If anyone has anything to get back at Doug for, it's me," Katie said. "I should have been on the baboons' side tonight. Christy, remember when we went on the houseboat, and Doug gave me a black eye?"

"That was an accident," Christy said unsympathetically.

"It's always an accident with him, but he's gotten me good more than once."

The light turned green, and Tracy drove on.

"What kind of a costume would they put on him?" Tawni asked.

"Whatever they could find," Tracy said.

"Or whatever they could afford," Christy suggested. "Gisele said she caught Larry calling around to costume shops last week. She didn't hear what kind of costume he was asking about, though."

"Oh great!" Tracy said. "He might very well be a big baboon! Poor Doug, riding the ferry all night in a costume. I sure hope he keeps his sense of humor."

"You think it's a baboon costume, really?" Katie asked.

"Who knows," said Tracy. "It could be a grass skirt and coconuts, knowing these guys."

"I bet it's a Raggedy Andy costume," Tawni said.

Everyone started to laugh.

"Why in the world would you say that?" Sierra asked.

"Because Jeremy's old roommate had a perfect Raggedy Andy costume. I saw a picture of him in it from a party he went to with his girlfriend. I bet they put Doug in that Raggedy Andy costume."

"He would have thrown the red wig into the water," Tracy said.

"And what's wrong with red hair?" Katie asked indignantly.

"Nothing. It's the wig. Doug hates anything restrictive on his head. He hardly ever wears hats. A wig would drive him crazy."

Turning onto a side street, Tracy expertly parallel-parked the car. The girls were so eager that they piled out before Tracy had even turned off the engine. The car that was following them parked at the end of the block, and the other girls hurried to catch up.

"Does anyone have any money?" Tracy asked. "We need fare for the ferry."

Heather said she had 20 dollars with her, enough to cover everyone. The girls took off in a rush, all talking at the same time.

"Do you have the camera?" Sierra asked.

"Yes. It's right here. Everyone stick together and watch out for these guys. They're sneaky."

They rounded the corner and saw a large crowd waiting for the next ferry, which was approaching from Balboa Island, a short distance away.

"Do you see any of the guys?" Christy asked.

"No," Katie said. "Maybe they're on the ferry."

The girls stood together, looking around and talking at full speed. Sierra fixed her eyes on the ferry coming toward them. When she had visited at Easter, she and some of her friends had ridden on it over to Balboa Island. She remembered the ferry was pretty small, just large enough to hold four cars. The journey took about 15 minutes.

It was dark across the water, yet plenty of light was supplied from the Ferris wheel and the Balboa Fun Zone Amusement Park to their right. As the ferry inched toward them, they saw a big yellow something in the front section.

"Tracy," Sierra said, tapping her shoulder, "what is that?"

Everyone looked to where Sierra pointed and squinted to see.

"Here he comes again," one of the men in the crowd ahead of them said. "Poor guy. I wonder if he's going to have to ride all night."

A man next to him said, "I heard someone say he's getting married this weekend. His girlfriend is supposed to come and make him promise not to chicken out."

The people around the girls all laughed.

"His fiancée is here," Katie said, loud enough for everyone to hear.

Now all eyes were on the girls, and the girls all looked at Tracy. She offered a weak smile to the curious crowd and gazed back out to sea.

"If I were you, I'd get while the going is good," one of the men said. "I heard someone say they were going to call the police."

"Oh no," Sierra heard Tracy mutter. "He's a big chicken."

"No, he's not," Christy said. "Doug is brave when it comes to difficult situations; you know that. The police will understand it's a prank."

"Christy," Sierra said, elbowing her and pointing to the big yellow blob in the front of the ferry. "Doug really is a chicken. He's a big yellow chicken. Look."

The ferry docked with a clunk, and poor Doug stood near the prow, dressed in a chicken costume, complete with a headdress, which Sierra imagined must be driving him crazy. He spotted them and called out, furiously waving his arms—or rather, his wings, "Trace! Over here! Hurry!"

All of them pushed through the crowd with quick apologies of "excuse me, pardon me" and dashed onto the ferry. Not one of the guys was anywhere to be seen. Doug's costume was a mass of bright-yellow feathers, detailed and authentic enough for him to qualify as half-time entertainment at a pro football game.

"Are you okay?" Tracy asked, reaching for his hand and catching her breath. A bowling ball was attached to the end of a heavy chain locked around Doug's ankle.

"Get this head thing off me. It's attached in the back, and I can't undo it with these wings."

Tracy fumbled with the clasps. "Help me, you guys."

Tawni was the first to jump in, then Christy.

"Fare please," the attendant said as the ferry pulled away from shore, towing them over to the island. He was a local beach boy with long, sun-bleached hair hanging in his eyes. He seemed unaffected by the chicken on board.

"Here. I have it," Heather said, paying for all of them.

"Where are the guys?" Katie asked.

"Don't move, Doug," Tawni said, fiddling with the costume. "I've got it. Bend your neck, and we can get this off you."

He cooperated gladly, and the giant feathered head and long orange beak pointed toward the ground. Within two minutes, Tawni had the monstrous chicken head off him. A red-faced, heavily perspiring Doug looked at her with gratitude.

"The guys are on the island waiting for us," Doug said.

"Oh yeah?" Katie said. "I want to see their faces when we pull up and show them we've freed you."

"I'm not going anywhere with this bowling ball around my ankle," Doug said. Turning to Tracy, he touched her cheek with his feathered hand and said, "Thanks for coming. Sorry if this interrupted your party."

"Don't worry about it," Tracy said. "Are you all right?" Two tiny yellow feathers stuck to her cheek.

"Much better now, thanks. I've been developing a bad case of claustrophobia the past hour. It feels good to breath clean air."

"You've been riding for an hour?" Tracy asked.

"I don't know. It feels like days."

"How are you going to take off the ball and chain?" Sierra asked. She knew she couldn't handle having something like that around her ankle. She would do better trapped inside the claustrophobic costume than be weighted down with a bowling ball around her foot— especially on a boat. The guys hadn't thought through how dangerous their prank could have turned if something had gone wrong on board.

"Larry has the combination to the lock," Doug said to Sierra. "Unless you feel like trying to figure out the combination, he'll have to get me off this big tub."

"I can do it," a man said. He was one of the many curious passengers on the ferry who had been observing the crazy scene. Without being invited, he knelt down by Doug's feet and put his ear to the lock. "Quiet, everyone!" he hollered. The stranger began to work the lock.

In less than two minutes, the man had the lock open. A spontaneous cheer rose from the girls and the observers. Katie, who was standing with Heather at the other end of the ferry, turned around to see what everyone was cheering about. Sierra considered joining them. She wanted to see the guys' reaction, too.

"This is what I do for a living," the man said, pushing up his glasses. "I'm a locksmith. Here's my card."

"May I pay you?" Doug said, slipping his foot out of the now open shackle.

"Nope. Consider it a wedding present. Just make sure you show up at the altar."

"No need to worry about that," Doug said.

Sierra noticed they were nearing the island. The guys had set up their own viewing area, complete with beach chairs, ice chest, and binoculars. She could see Larry standing in the middle of them with his hands cupped over his mouth.

He called out, "Why did the chicken cross the bay?"

"I thought they would have run out of those jokes by now," Doug muttered. He had unzipped the back of the chicken suit and was stepping out of it. His T-shirt and shorts were soaked with sweat. "Now it's time for me to play a little joke on them," he said, crouching behind one of the cars.

"Here, Tawni. Hide this." He handed her the big fluffy costume.

"Hide it? Where?"

"And Sierra, when I give the signal, you throw the ball and chain into the water. Ready?"

Sierra lifted the heavy ball. The ferry nosed its way into the dock, and Doug hid himself in a shadow at the edge of the deck. Grinning, he climbed onto the railing.

"Doug," Tracy yelled, rushing over to him, "what are you doing?"

"Playing the best trick of my life," he whispered.

Chapter Thirteen

THE FERRY DOCKED, AND DOUG YELLED, "I can't take this anymore!" Then, with a quick nod to Sierra, he jumped feet first into the bay.

Sierra was startled for a moment. Then she remembered his instructions and threw the bowling ball into the water, far away from where Doug had jumped.

Tracy let out a loud shriek.

Larry bellowed, "What's he doing? There's a bowling ball on his leg!"

Katie immediately ran back to where Sierra and Tracy stood and frantically yelled, "Isn't anyone going to do something?"

Before they could stop her, Katie whipped off her jacket and scrambled over the side of the ferry into the water.

"You guys can't do that!" the ferry pilot called out to the swimmers. The pilot threw up his arms in frustration as Todd and Jeremy ran onto the ferry, with Larry and the other guys right behind them.

"It's okay!" Christy yelled to them.

"He didn't have the bowling ball on!" Sierra yelled.

"It was supposed to be a joke!" Tracy yelled.

Todd leaped over the side and swam over to Katie.

"I can't find him!" Katie screamed, surfacing in a panic.

"It's okay," Todd said, coming up beside her and shouting for her to calm down. "Doug is playing a joke on us."

"He is?" Katie treaded water and looked around.

From Sierra's vantage point, the water looked disgusting. It had a thin film of oil on the surface that caught the lights from the shore and made wobbly, distorted rings around Todd and Katie.

"Then where is he?" Katie cried out, scanning her surroundings.

Todd immediately dove down to look while Katie kept treading water.

"Is he on the other side?" Katie called out.

Tracy and Christy dashed to the other side of the ferry and searched the water, along with a dozen onlookers who hadn't exited yet.

Leaning out of his control booth, the captain said to Sierra, "Is there somebody still in the water? They can't do that."

"Three people are in the water. One of them hasn't surfaced yet, though," Sierra responded.

"That's it. I'm making the call," the captain said and ducked back inside.

"Doug!" Tracy screamed. "Doug!"

"Is he over there?" Tawni asked, her voice filled with panic.

Jeremy had his arm around her, and they were looking back and forth across both sides of the water.

Tracy screamed out again, "Doug, this isn't funny!"

"I'm over here," a voice called from the side of the ferry where Sierra stood. She scanned the water but couldn't see anyone.

"Tracy, he's over here!" Sierra called out.

Immediately, two dozen people ran to that side of the ferry.

"What are you doing?!" Tracy yelled into the dark water. "Where are you? I can't see you!"

Todd surfaced, and Christy cried out, "Todd, he's okay. He's in the water somewhere."

"Where?" Katie asked, her head bobbing. Suddenly, a glaring searchlight shone from the side of the ferry, lighting up the water and revealing the heads of Todd, Katie, and far to the side, Doug.

"All right," the captain called through his bullhorn, "everyone out of the water. Now! I've called the authorities. This prank has gone on too long. Get out now."

Katie and Todd swam toward the shore, but Doug didn't move.

The light shone on him, and the captain called, "Get out of the water immediately."

"I'd like to," Doug said as the large audience on the ferry and on the shore watched him in the spotlight. "But you see I, um . . . I seem to have lost my shorts somewhere here in the water and ah . . ."

The audience burst out laughing. Someone took a picture.

The locksmith stepped up next to Sierra and said, "Here. I have an extra pair."

He unzipped the small gym bag he had with him and threw a pair of swim trunks to Doug.

Everyone watched while Doug grabbed the trunks and then maneuvered underwater to get them on.

Katie and Todd were scrambling up the sharp rocks by the dock, trying to get out of the water. Suddenly, Katie let out a cry of pain. Sierra thought she heard Katie say, "My foot." But so much noise and confusion filled the air that it was hard to tell. The cars on the shore side were honking to get onto the ferry, a siren wailed as a police car tried to get through behind them, and everyone was heckling Doug as he dog-paddled toward the rocks.

"Come on," Tawni said. "Let's get off the boat."

She and Jeremy led the way, with Sierra, Tracy, and Christy right behind. The other guys from the group and three of the other girls were already off the ferry. They had gathered around the rocks, where Todd was trying to help Katie get up on the level ground.

When Sierra arrived, she could see that Katie was in serious pain. She was lying on her side, soaking wet, shivering, and holding her ankle.

"Try not to move it," Todd said, leaning over her, dripping wet.

"What happened?" Christy yelled over the siren, which was now right behind them.

"She caught her foot between the rocks," Todd said. He flipped his hair back in his surfer fashion, sending droplets everywhere.

"I twisted it," Katie said between gasps for breath. "Ouch! It really hurts."

Sierra noticed that the vehicle with the siren was an ambulance, not a police car.

Larry motioned to the paramedic and called out, "Over here."

The crowd seemed to grow larger as the paramedic bent over Katie and began to ask her questions. Doug, who was safely out of the water and wearing the loaned swim trunks, which were too small for him, stood beside Todd. Christy and Tracy had joined them, but Sierra hung back with Tawni, Jeremy, and some of their friends.

"This turned out to be a mess," Tawni said. She held the bulky chicken costume in front of her.

"Maybe we should go back to Doug's house," Jeremy suggested. "Or were you planning to go back to Tracy's?"

"I think we should go to Tracy's, as long as Katie is okay."

One of the girls from their group ventured over to the thick of the action and returned to say the paramedics were taking Katie to the hospital. It was possible her foot was broken.

"That's awful," Sierra said. "Isn't she supposed to be in the wedding?"

"Not really," Tawni said. "Christy is the maid of honor, and Katie was going to do the guest book, I think."

"She might end up on crutches," Sierra speculated.

"I'm sure she'll find a way to blame it on Doug," Heather said.

"Well, if he hadn't jumped in . . . ," Tawni said in Katie's defense. "She was acting out of concern. Obviously, she didn't know he had taken off the bowling ball."

"That shouldn't matter," Jeremy said. "Why would it be Doug's fault? Katie didn't have to go flying into the water like some superhero. Why did she feel responsible to save Doug?"

"That's the way she is," Sierra interjected, hoping to calm the brewing argument between Jeremy and Tawni. "Same with Todd. The two of them respond quickly in a crisis and then think about it later."

"If you ask me," Tawni said, "Doug was the one who wasn't thinking. It was a bad move for him to try to pull off this joke. He practically scared Tracy to death. I bet she's furious with him."

Tawni was right. Tracy *was* furious.

Katie was taken to the hospital, and Christy and Todd went along in the ambulance. The rest of the group gathered back at Tracy's house; anger was written all over Tracy's usually sweet face. Her mom invited them to come in and have some cake. Tracy was the only one who didn't eat any.

Doug didn't seem to take the incident too lightly

either. He kept looking at Tracy as if hoping for a sign that she had calmed down.

"I think the locksmith was your guardian angel," Heather told Doug. "I mean, how many guys do you know who can open a lock like that and just happen to have an extra pair of shorts with them?"

"What a ridiculous notion!" Marti spouted. "How absurd to think God would send help to save you from your own foolishness."

Doug immediately spoke up in agreement with her. "It was foolish. I can say before everyone here—" He looked at Tracy and attempted a sincere smile. "I learned my lesson tonight. I'm finished with practical jokes. It's no fun when someone gets hurt. Or scared," he added.

"I should say not," Marti agreed. "I'm ready to go home. Who is going with me?"

Sierra looked around. She was the only one left of the group that had ridden over with Marti. Katie and Christy were still at the hospital, and Tawni and Jeremy had left earlier, since they had a long ride down the coast. "I guess I am," she said.

All the way home, Marti vented her concerns and frustrations about Christy's friends' foolishness. "It's time they grew up," Marti said. "You're new to this group, so you don't know them the way I do, Sierra. I've known these young people for years. It's absolutely ridiculous the way they carry on like immature teenagers. It's a good thing Robert wasn't there tonight. I'm sure my foolish husband would have been right in the middle of it all."

Marti pressed the garage door opener. "This only proves what I've thought all along. Christy must go away to school, or Todd will never mature. That young man hardly has an ounce of responsibility in his body."

Sierra thought of how Todd had turned down the invitation to go to Switzerland because he couldn't take any more time off from work. That sounded pretty responsible to her.

"There's no reason Christy shouldn't go to school in Europe. I can't understand why she would even consider passing up such an opportunity, to stay around here with friends like that."

"Don't you like Todd?" Sierra asked as Marti turned off the engine.

Marti looked shocked. "Of course! We love Todd like our own son. How can you ask such a thing?"

Sierra shrugged.

"My concern is for Christina. She is not the kind of woman who should marry young. This is her chance to see the world. Otherwise, she will regret it years later."

Sierra wasn't sure how Marti had come up with such logic. *I wonder how old Marti was when she and Bob married.* Sierra decided she had better not say anything, so she focused on keeping her lips sealed as they went inside.

On the kitchen counter was a note from Bob, saying he had received a call from Todd and had gone to the hospital.

"Who knows when they'll be back," Marti said. "I'm going to bed. Please make yourself at home."

"Thank you," Sierra said. "Good night."

"It's been a night, all right," Marti muttered. "If those two ever make it to the altar, I'll be amazed."

Sierra didn't know if Marti was referring to Doug and Tracy or to Todd and Christy.

Chapter Fourteen

THE NEXT DAY SPED BY IN A WILD AND colorful blur. Katie and Christy had arrived home from the hospital late the night before when Sierra was already asleep. In the morning, Katie modeled the cast on her right foot and asked Sierra to sign it. Despite the trauma of the night before, Katie was in good spirits.

The phone rang all morning with calls from friends checking in on Katie. Of course, everyone had to go over his or her version of what had happened. Heather told them it was in the paper. Christy and Sierra ran downstairs to find the story, leaving Katie limping behind.

The write-up was on the second page of the local news section and consisted of nine lines describing a prank played by some college students on their friend who was getting married. The last line said, "Police Chief Sanders warned that such activities can be dangerous, as was evidenced by one of the teens being taken to the hospital with a broken leg."

"Foot," Katie corrected Christy as she read the article aloud in the kitchen. "I'm going to call them and tell them it was a broken foot, not a broken leg."

Before she had the opportunity to make good on her threat, the phone rang. Bob took it and went into the other room.

The three girls were still in their nightshirts when Sierra noticed the time. "It's almost noon, you guys. We should probably get dressed soon."

"It can't be that late!" Christy said. "I have to be at the church at 4:00 for the dress rehearsal, and then at 6:00, there's a fancy dinner for the wedding party and relatives. I still don't know what I'm going to wear, and I need to call my parents."

Christy spent close to an hour on the phone with her parents, discussing Marti's plans for the Switzerland trip, which only seemed to stress Christy out more. She talked Sierra into ironing a blouse for her while she jumped into the shower.

Katie hopped around on her crutches but seemed to have lost some of her spring. The cast went up to her knee and had to be uncomfortable; also, she was probably still dealing with the trauma of having a broken bone.

Marti fluttered around the house, worrying about everything for everyone. Did Todd pick up his tux yet? Should they call Tracy's mom to see if she needed help on any last-minute details?

Marti followed Sierra up to the guest bedroom, where she put the freshly ironed blouse on a hanger in the closet.

Katie had stretched out on the bed and propped up her foot with some pillows.

"What about Doug?" Marti continued her worry-fest. "Should Bob call him to make sure he has picked up the ring from the jeweler? And what about the marriage license? Todd and Christy will be required to sign it tomorrow as the witnesses. Do you think Doug will remember to bring it to the church?"

Marti finally left Christy, Katie, and Sierra alone in the bedroom when she realized she hadn't called her favorite department store to make sure the wedding gift had been delivered to Tracy's house.

"Remind me to elope," Christy said, towel-drying her long, nutmeg-colored hair.

"Oh?" Katie said. "Is this something we should start reminding you of very soon?"

"No." Christy stepped back into the adjoining bathroom and turned on the hair dryer.

Katie and Sierra exchanged glances.

"I give them six months," Katie said.

"What if she goes to Switzerland?" Sierra asked.

"She won't go. Would you?"

"Yes, I definitely would," Sierra said.

"So would I, but Christy won't. She's hasn't been bitten by the same adventure bug that got you and me."

"I heard that," Christy said, turning off the blow dryer. "And for your information, I think I'm going to go."

"You are?" Katie and Sierra said in unison.

Christy stepped back into the bedroom and said

calmly, "I think I'm going to go with my aunt to check things out next week. I asked my mom to go with us, and she's going to talk to Dad about it. They'll be at the wedding tomorrow night, and she said she would tell me then. If Mom goes, then I'll go."

"Rats," Katie said. "I was hoping you would take me."

"Oh, I'm sure you would have a lot of fun hopping around Europe on crutches."

"Hey, it's not as bad as that girl in the *Heidi* movie. What was her name? The rich one from the city? She managed to get around the Alps in a wheelchair."

"Yes," said Christy with a laugh, "but she had Heidi and the grandfather to push her around, and all you would have is Aunt Marti and me."

Just then the door swung open, and Marti blew in, her face pink. Sierra wondered if she had a radar that could detect when they were joking about her.

"I've canceled my account at that store," she said. "I ordered two settings of Doug and Tracy's china, and the store told me they delivered everything but the salad plates."

Sierra and Katie looked at each other. This did not seem like a tragedy.

"Only, just now they informed me that the salad plates are, in fact, in stock and available if I'd like to come down and get them myself. That means, if Doug and Tracy are going to receive the complete set, I have to pick them up. Who wants to go with me?"

Again Sierra and Katie exchanged glances. Then Sierra and Christy looked at each other.

"I need to finish getting ready for the rehearsal," Christy said. "I have to leave in less than an hour."

"My foot has been kind of sore," Katie said.

Sierra felt a tightening in her chest. She didn't want to go with Marti, someone she didn't particularly enjoy, on this stressful mission. Sierra knew if Doug and Tracy's wedding was anything like her brother Cody's, they wouldn't even open the presents until after they came back from their honeymoon. She was certain the salad plates would not be missed.

"Can't you ask the store to deliver them?" Sierra asked calmly. "I mean, didn't they deliver the rest of the china to Tracy's house? They should be able to deliver the salad plates, too. If not today, then certainly by tomorrow."

"That's right," Katie said. "And tell them to do a gift wrap."

Marti's worry-creased forehead began to smooth out. "I think you're right. Why should I have to pick up the salad plates? The store made the mistake, not me. I'm going to call them right back and tell them exactly that."

She breezed out of the room, leaving Katie, Christy, and Sierra to exchange glances.

"Yep," Katie said, stretching her hands behind her head. "Like I was saying, I hope you and your mother have a delightful time in the Alps with Aunt Marti. You couldn't pay Sierra or me to endure that nonstop for a week."

"Oh, I don't know," Sierra said. "Maybe if the price was right."

There was a tap on the door.

"Come in," Christy called out.

Uncle Bob poked his head around the open door. "Everybody decent?"

"Yes."

"Christy, Todd's here."

"Already? We're not supposed to leave for almost another hour."

"Well, it seems he hasn't purchased a wedding gift yet, and he thought maybe you could go shopping with him before the rehearsal."

Katie started to giggle. "Tell him to get on the phone with Marti right now, and he can chip in for some lovely salad plates. Or maybe the matching gravy boat hasn't been purchased yet."

"Katie, be nice," Christy said. "Uncle Bob, could you please tell Todd I'll be ready in about 15 minutes, but we'll have to go shopping for a present tomorrow morning."

"Got it," Bob said, bowing like a gracious butler.

"Oh, wait!" Christy said. "What's Todd wearing?"

"Standard apparel for a beach bum."

"I was afraid of that. Could you also remind him this is a dressy occasion? He probably should go home to change."

"As you wish," Bob said with a smile, closing the door behind him.

"He's been to weddings before," Christy muttered, bending over and lowering her head so that her damp hair hung almost to the floor. She began to vigorously brush the underside. "I can't believe he thought he could show up in shorts and thongs."

"Are you sure it's formal?" Katie said. "My brother's wedding rehearsal was very casual." Before Sierra or Christy could comment, Katie answered herself. "But then my brother got married in a park in Reno, and the rehearsal dinner was at the Blackjack Buffet at the Starlight Motel."

Sierra started to laugh. "Are you serious?"

Katie nodded but didn't elaborate. Sierra decided it was best not to laugh.

Bob tapped again on the door and entered. "Mission accomplished," he said. "Todd will be back in 45 minutes with bells on."

"Bells?" Christy questioned. "I'll be happy if he manages to find a pair of dress slacks and a clean shirt." Turning to Sierra and Katie, she said, "Is that too much to ask?"

Neither of them dared to answer.

Uncle Bob left, and Christy went to work on her makeup while Katie and Sierra discussed Christy's outfit options for the evening. They finally agreed on a simple short skirt and a different top than the one Sierra had ironed. It was a nice basic outfit that Katie convinced Christy would work well with either a casual or dressy escort.

Sierra admired Christy's calm response to everything that had been thrown at her all afternoon. She looked like the picture of repose and sweetness as she leaned toward the bathroom mirror to run the mascara brush over her eyelashes. Sierra wanted to be like that. Mild-mannered and happy in a deep, settled way.

"What are you two going to do all night?" Christy asked.

"Oh, we thought we would go roller blading," Katie joked. "Then maybe do a little jogging along the beach. Maybe join the neighborhood kids for some street hockey. You know, the usual."

Christy laughed. "Well, whatever you do, have fun." She swished out the door, leaving a faint scent of green-apple hair spray behind her.

"So what do you want to do?" Sierra asked Katie.

"I don't know. What do you want to do?"

Sierra laughed. "You know, we're pathetic."

"No we're not. Let's talk Bob into taking us somewhere."

"Okay. Where?"

"I don't care. Any place that doesn't discriminate against one-legged redheads."

Sierra laughed. "Come on. Let's go coax him together. I have a feeling you have more experience at this than I do."

"You know it," Katie said, reaching for her crutches. "Come with me, Sierra, and I shall teach you the fine art of persuasion. Our target is the shy and unsuspecting Uncle Bob."

Chapter Fifteen

SIERRA TURNED OVER AND PULLED THE COVERS up to her chin. She wiggled her feet and tried to get comfortable. The dark guest room was quiet except for the gentle ruffle of Katie's breathing.

It was after midnight, but Christy wasn't back yet. Sierra felt like a mother hen, worrying about her. Was she with Todd? Were they discussing her choice about school in Switzerland? Or was the wedding party playing some more practical jokes on Doug and Tracy?

Sierra and Katie had spent an uneventful evening going out to dinner with Bob and Marti and coming back to their house to watch TV. Apparently, Katie's art of persuasion was still in the training stages when it came to Uncle Bob. Of course, he was affected by Marti, who was still anxious about the wedding. She had spent most of dinner thinking of things they should worry about just in case no one else had thought of them yet. Marti had gone so far as to worry whether the air conditioning would be turned on inside the reception hall so the cake wouldn't get mushy and tumble over.

Katie and Sierra had headed upstairs to bed at 11:00, but since they had slept in so late that morning, Sierra couldn't sleep now. She thought about Amy and wondered what was happening with Nathan. Hopefully, Amy had listened to Sierra's message and would understand what Sierra was trying to say.

What concerned Sierra most was that Amy's parents were having marriage difficulties, which seemed to make Amy eager for attention and love. Sierra hoped Amy wouldn't compromise her standards with a guy like Nathan in order to get the affection she craved.

Sierra heard soft footsteps coming up the stairs. The door opened slowly, and Christy tiptoed into the room.

"It's okay," Sierra whispered. "I'm still awake. Katie's asleep, but I don't think you could wake her if you tried. How did everything go?"

Christy followed the dim glow of the night-light and sat on the edge of Sierra's bed.

"It went well," she whispered. "I think everything will go smoothly tomorrow. It was so sweet when we were practicing and the pastor reached the part 'you may kiss the bride.' Doug took Tracy in his arms, and I thought he was going to kiss her! But he just looked into her eyes about an inch away from her face. I mean to tell you, Sierra, it was about the most romantic, totally make-you-melt scene in the world. Then I heard him whisper to her, 'Tomorrow, my love. Tomorrow.'"

Sierra smiled in the darkness. "This first-kiss pledge is really a huge thing for Doug, isn't it?"

"I think it's become big for all of us. Doug is sort of our group's symbol of purity. If he had kissed her tonight, I think I would have been mad at him. They would have come so close to their goal and then missed it by a few hours."

"Christy," Sierra said slowly, "is it strange for you to see Doug and Tracy getting married since you used to date Doug?"

"No." Christy paused before she continued. "In some ways, it doesn't seem like I ever dated Doug. I mean, he was more my friend, my buddy. We did a lot of things together, and I know he enjoyed being with me, but there wasn't any twinkle dust between us."

"Twinkle dust?"

Christy quietly giggled. "I don't know what else to call it. Sometimes when I look at Todd, it's as if God sprinkled a handful of golden glitter in the air that hangs between us. Nobody can see it but us. It connects us—strongly. I know there is twinkle dust between Doug and Tracy. They are going to be very happy together."

"Does that mean Tracy got over being mad at Doug about what happened last night?"

"I think so. She was pretty mad, though. I heard him say again tonight to his mom that his days of boyish pranks are over."

"Katie will be glad to hear that," Sierra said.

"I think you're right." A yawn escaped from Christy. "I'd better let you get some sleep," she said. "Sweet dreams."

She rose and headed into the bathroom, quietly closing the door. Sierra drew back the cover because now she was too warm.

Twinkle dust, she thought. *I like that.*

A contented smile rested on her lips as she drifted off to sleep. It seemed she couldn't stop smiling the next morning either. It didn't matter that Aunt Marti was in a high-strung lather over her worries. When Christy left to go shopping with Todd, it didn't bother Sierra to stay behind with Katie. Nor did it seem irritating that Katie, who was more uncomfortable today, kept asking Sierra to do little things for her. Sierra felt happy—happy deep down. She thought about Tracy all morning and wondered if she was feeling immensely joyful or if she was being driven crazy by everyone and everything.

Sierra thought nothing could rob her of all this happiness. After taking a long shower, she stepped into the bedroom with a towel wrapped around her, ready to put on the one nice outfit she had brought along for the wedding.

Katie, who was standing by the bed where Sierra had laid out her outfit, immediately said, "I'm sorry, Sierra. It was an accident."

"What was an accident?"

"Your skirt. It got caught on the bottom of my crutch, and when I pulled it away, it ripped in three different directions. I'm so sorry. I don't think it can be fixed. Do you have anything else to wear?"

Sierra rushed over and examined the thin gauze skirt.

She felt an angry frustration surging inside. First Amy had ripped her blue skirt and now this.

"No," she said sharply, "this is all I brought."

She had thrown in plenty of casual clothes when she had packed in her flurry, but she hadn't thought through her need for dressy outfits. Her thoughts had been fixed on her visit here at Easter when all she needed were shorts and sweatshirts.

"I feel awful," Katie said.

"Maybe I can sew it," Sierra suggested. Whenever she had thought about Doug and Tracy's wedding during the past few weeks, this was the outfit she had pictured herself wearing. It truly reflected her personality.

"I don't think there's time. Christy left with Todd while you were in the shower, and Marti said she wanted to leave early. I told her you weren't ready, so she went with Todd and Christy. Bob is downstairs waiting for us."

"What time is it?" Sierra asked.

"It's almost 6:00."

"The wedding isn't until 7:00," Sierra said, examining the huge rip more closely. She knew gauze wasn't the sturdiest fabric, but still, why did all her clothes have to get ruined? She had only so many favorites.

"I know, but I'm supposed to be there early to stand by the guest book. Are you sure you don't have anything else you could wear?"

"I'm sure," Sierra said. It was depressing to realize how important her style had become to her and how devastated she felt when that foundation was rocked.

"This is all I brought," Katie said, looking down at her simple, forest-green dress. "Maybe Christy has something. Check her suitcase."

"I couldn't borrow her clothes," Sierra said.

"Don't worry. She'll understand."

She may understand, but I won't be me if I'm dressed like Christy. You're the one who doesn't understand, Katie, Sierra fumed silently.

Katie hobbled over to Christy's suitcase and bent down to open it up. "Look, here's a dress right on top. Try this on. It might be a little big on you, but it's better than a pair of shorts, which is all I have to offer you."

Sierra took one look at the dress and tried not to grimace. It was a pastel yellow with sweet little flowers sprinkled all over it and a little bow at the neckline. Fine for Christy, but definitely not something Sierra would ever choose to wear in public.

"I don't know," Sierra said, stalling.

"We don't have any other options," Katie said, rifling through Christy's clothes.

Sierra looked at her skirt again and wondered if she could turn the tear to the back or to the side. Then it wouldn't be so obvious.

Why am I being so stubborn about this? I'm not usually obsessed with clothes. Am I?

It occurred to Sierra that her trademark had been her distinctive outfits. In England, it had been her dad's old cowboy boots. Even Paul had commented on them. No one referred to her as "the young one" but as "the girl with the creative clothes." When she had met Amy the first day of school, they were drawn together by their similar patchwork outfits and their love of shopping at thrift stores and vintage shops. Sierra's clothes had become her identity.

A friendly tap sounded on the bedroom door. "How's it going in there, ladies?" Bob asked through the closed door. "We should be heading over there now."

Sierra looked at Katie and then at the dress.

"We're coming," she called to Bob.

She scooped up the dress and returned to the bathroom. Two minutes later, humbled and still a little frustrated, Sierra emerged wearing the yellow dress.

"You look adorable," Katie said with a congenial grin.

"My worst nightmare is that I would grow up to look adorable," Sierra said, shaking her wet locks. "Let me grab some jewelry and my shoes."

"What about your hair?" Katie asked.

"What about it?"

"You don't need to dry it or anything?"

"Nope. This is as good as it gets. I gave up on it long ago."

"I love your hair," Katie said. "It's like the symbol of a free-spirited woman."

Sierra had to laugh. Here she had thought her trademark was her clothes. "I'm a free-spirited woman who happens to be wearing a little posy dress. Is there something wrong with this picture?"

Katie kept assuring Sierra she looked fine. All the way

to the church, Katie talked about how if there was one thing she had learned in life, it was that your true friends love you no matter what. And the only people who qualify for true, true friends are those who pay attention to what a person is like on the inside.

"I think you're right, Katie," Bob agreed. He pulled out an index card from the black leather daily planner on the seat next to him. "Sounds a little like my quote for the week. Do you want to hear it? This is by Augustine: 'O soul, He only who created thee can satisfy thee. If thou ask for anything else, it is thy misfortune, for He alone who made thee in His image can satisfy thee.' That's rich, isn't it?"

"Read it again," Katie said.

Bob glanced from the road to the card and back to the road.

"Wait," Katie said. "Maybe you'd better read it, Sierra."

She was sitting next to Bob in the front seat. He handed her the card, and she read the quote.

"It's true, you know," Bob said when she finished. "It was my misfortune to spend nearly half a century looking for anything and everything that might satisfy me. I know now that only God can fill an empty soul."

For a quiet moment, Sierra and Katie absorbed his wisdom.

"Here we are," Bob said, breaking the serious moment as he pulled into the church parking lot. "This is the first wedding I've gone to as a believer."

They got out of the car, and Bob, still smiling, added, "I think I'm more excited about this wedding than anyone else is."

"Oh, don't count on it," Katie said, motioning to the steady stream of cars pouring into the parking lot. "This is going to be a wedding worth remembering."

I'll remember it, all right, Sierra thought ruefully. *I'll always remember this as the wedding I went to in a borrowed yellow dress with a bow on it.*

Chapter Sixteen

As soon as Sierra, Bob, and Katie reached the front of the church, it became obvious Katie was late for her job as guest-book attendant. People were lined up to sign the book, and Marti was accommodating them by standing next to the podium and handing them the white feathered pen.

"Katie, I'm so glad you're here." Marti's voice was like syrup: sweet and sticky. "Thank you," she said to a guest handing back the long plume.

Katie and Sierra slipped past the guests and went to Marti's side. "You sure you want me to take over? You look like you're having fun," Katie said.

"This is your job." Marti handed the pen to the next guest with a smile and a nod. "However, if you think you might have difficulty managing it . . ."

"Maybe I'll just stand here and greet everyone with you," Katie suggested. As soon as she spoke, though, she recognized someone in line and squealed, "Stephanie, I didn't know you were coming!"

Marti cringed visibly at Katie's loud voice, shaking her

head in disapproval as Katie left her post and made her way over to give the girl in line a hug.

Sierra wasn't sure if she should get in line to sign the guest book or find Bob, who had disappeared. She carried her gift over to the gift table, where one of Tracy's aunts who had been at the shower greeted Sierra warmly and took the gift from her. Sierra hoped Tracy and Doug would like the teapot. It seemed like a simple gift compared with Marti's china place settings and the silver tea service from Tracy's grandma that they had used at the shower.

It's from my heart, and that's what matters most, she reminded herself.

Sierra stood to the side and watched all the people enter the church's narthex. Bob was talking to Todd, and Sierra smiled when she saw Todd, the beach bum, dressed in a black tux. All the ushers were guys Sierra had met, and all of them were surfers, transformed in their formal wear—especially Larry, who was the largest guy Sierra had ever known. She wondered if it had been hard to find a tux big enough to fit him. He certainly looked good in it.

Tawni and Jeremy stood together at the guest book, and Marti gave Tawni a kiss that touched the air beside Tawni's cheek. Sierra walked over to join them.

"Hi," Tawni said, looking Sierra over with an expression of pleasant surprise. "You look nice. Is that a new dress?"

Sierra swallowed a scream. "Not exactly." Wearing something that her sister approved of was not something

Sierra normally did. Actually, it was a dreaded thought. Tawni's approval meant that Sierra had sold out her unique style and become like everyone else. She couldn't do that. She had to remain unique and be noticed for it.

When Sierra didn't offer any more explanation about the dress, Jeremy asked, "Should we sit on the bride's side or the groom's side?"

"I don't think it matters when you're friends with both of them," Tawni said.

"Maybe not," Jeremy said, "but let's ask one of these guys in the monkey suits."

He led Tawni by the hand over to Todd and said to him, "What are you doing out here? Isn't the best man supposed to be back there making sure the groom doesn't pass out or something?"

Todd laughed. "They didn't need me, that's for sure. Doug had enough photographers and fathers and grand-fathers and uncles with him to keep him busy until the organ cranks up." He smiled at Tawni and Sierra, giving them both a chin-up nod.

"That's a nice dress," he said to Sierra.

She clenched her teeth and forced herself to smile. "It's vaguely familiar, don't you think?"

Todd didn't catch her comment because a tall, good-looking guy with dark, wavy hair and chocolate-brown eyes strode up to their little group and gave Todd a punch in the arm.

"Hey, Moon Doggie," he said sarcastically. "What's up, dude?"

Todd gave him a punch back and said, "Hey, dude! How you been? I heard you were getting married."

"No, not me," the guy said, turning to check out Sierra and Tawni. It felt like a visual x-ray.

"You know Jeremy," Todd said. "This is Sierra and Tawni Jensen."

The guy gave Sierra a polite nod. Then he offered his hand to Tawni and held it just a little too long, Sierra thought.

"This is Rick Doyle," Todd said. "We go way back."

"Christy's here, isn't she?" Rick asked.

Todd nodded. "She's the maid of honor. You won't be able to miss her."

"And you two are still . . . ?" Rick tilted his head and looked at Todd.

Todd didn't reply. He stood his ground with his arms folded across his chest, waiting for Rick to complete his question. Sierra thought she saw a hint of laughter in Todd's silver-blue eyes.

"Never mind," Rick said, throwing up his hands. "Why do I bother to ask?"

"Beats me," Todd said.

"Beats you," Rick repeated under his breath, letting out a huff. "Like I ever could."

"I think we should probably go inside," Tawni suggested.

"Good idea," Rick said. He held out his arm to Tawni, inviting her to take it and let him usher her down the aisle.

Tawni refused his offer by turning from him and

taking Jeremy's arm. Rick recovered flawlessly from Tawni's snub, and for a moment, Sierra thought he was about to make the same offer to her.

Before Rick had a chance, though, Todd stepped in, and in a calm, steady voice, he said, "May I escort you to your seat, Sierra?"

She slipped her hand into the crook of his tuxedoed arm and let Todd usher her down the aisle on the bride's side. He stopped about six rows back, and Sierra took little steps in until she was next to Jeremy. Tawni was on the aisle.

A thick white satin ribbon roped off the end of the pew from the center aisle. Bright nosegays of summer flowers were gathered in the middle of white bows on the end of each pew. A long white runner went down the middle of the church and came to an abrupt halt at the altar.

As tender piano music filled the air, Sierra could feel her heart beating a little faster in this beautiful, holy place. She drew in the heady fragrance of the flowers. Two tall wicker baskets at the front of the church spilled over with a colorful assortment of roses, carnations, statice, and ivy. A brass archway laced with ivy and roses stood between the two flower arrangements. Sprinkles of baby's breath dotted the ivy and flowers, giving it a touch-of-heaven look. In front of the archway stood a kneeling bench covered in white satin.

"Have you seen the dresses yet?" Tawni asked, leaning over Jeremy and whispering to Sierra.

She shook her head.

"Me neither. I wonder what they'll look like, because I know she wanted a garden theme. It's beautiful, isn't it?" Tawni asked.

Sierra nodded.

More guests entered in a steady stream. All the aisle seats and the first five rows were packed. Now the ushers were filling in the row where Sierra sat. She turned to see that the guest who lowered himself into the place next to her was Rick. Giving him only the slightest nod and smile, Sierra looked back toward the front of the sanctuary. She shifted in her seat and found she had involuntarily moved a pinch closer to Jeremy and farther away from Rick. Sierra didn't know why, but he gave her a creepy feeling. She usually was a good judge of character, and this was one guy she didn't like.

The church continued to fill with guests.

Rick leaned over, his musk-scented aftershave coming too close to Sierra's nose for her liking. "Looks like this is the event of the century," he murmured.

Sierra didn't feel compelled to respond.

"You would think they were the only two people who ever decided to get married," Rick mumbled in Sierra's ear. "There must be 300 people here. And there's more coming. What a mob! You think they're all here to see Doug's lips finally lose their virginity?"

Without turning her head, Sierra stated flatly, "Well, it must be a sight worth seeing. You're here, aren't you?"

She heard no sound from Rick in response. About a minute later, he stood and, excusing himself, stepped over people all the way to the side aisle. Then he disappeared into the narthex.

"What did you say to him?" Jeremy whispered.

Sierra shrugged and used her eyes to convey her innocence to Jeremy.

He smiled at her and said, "Don't give me that." He tilted his head and looked at Sierra with the same kind of tender big-brother look Wesley gave her. "I probably shouldn't tell you this . . . ."

He paused and glanced at Tawni. She was watching the people being seated across the aisle. Sierra noticed that Rick was one of them. He had found some other, more attentive young woman to sit beside.

Jeremy looked at Sierra again and said, "Tawni told me I should tell you, but I wasn't sure."

"What?" Sierra said. Her curiosity was stirred by the look on Jeremy's face. He seemed tender and concerned. She couldn't imagine what it was he wanted to tell her.

Just then the piano music stopped. All eyes went to the front as the minister stepped out from a side door. Facing the wedding guests, he positioned himself between the altar and the kneeling bench under the garden arch.

Sierra knew Jeremy couldn't finish his sentence now, but it didn't matter. Right behind the pastor, in a straight line, came Doug followed by Todd and two other groomsmen. They all wore black tuxes. Doug's had long tails; a single white rose adorned his lapel. He stood to the right of the garden arch and turned to face the guests with his hands folded in front of him.

Sierra had never seen a face brimming with so much dignity and honor. Clearly, Doug took this ceremony seriously. She knew no goofy smiles or gestures would be exchanged with the groomsmen as she had seen in other weddings. Doug's expression made it clear this was a holy moment between himself, his bride, and the Lord.

A reverent hush fell over the sanctuary.

Chapter Seventeen

SUDDENLY, THE SILENCE WAS BROKEN AS THE pianist began to play a lilting classical piece that Sierra vaguely recognized. As the song filled the air, Doug's parents were ushered in, with Tracy's mom and grandparents following.

An angelic little girl wearing a wreath of flowers in her blond hair started down the center aisle, one foot placed carefully in front of the other. She held a tiny garden basket in her hand. Halfway down the aisle, she remembered to take out some of the pink rose petals and sprinkle them on the white runner. Her task seemed to become more difficult as she dropped the flowers. Step, stop, take out one petal, drop it. Step, stop, repeat the one-petal drop.

People were smiling, whispering, and craning their necks to see the flower girl dutifully complete her journey to the front of the church. She received a subtle wink from Doug when she reached her goal. Then, with continued careful little steps, she made her way to her post.

The first bridesmaid, a relative of Tracy's, began her

slow walk down the aisle with the music lifting into the air. She wore a long, flowing gossamer dress in pale lavender and a wreath of flowers and ivy around her head. Instead of a bouquet of flowers, she held what Granna Mae called a gathering basket. It had a long, flat bottom made for collecting cut flowers from the garden. From this bridesmaid's gathering basket tumbled a cascade of summer garden flowers. Sierra thought it was clever and exactly like Tracy to think of something so creative.

The second bridesmaid made her way down the aisle in the same outfit, only her dress was a pale pink. Then came Christy in pale blue. Her long hair hung over her shoulders, curled perfectly on the ends. The wreath of flowers around her head was thicker than the other girls'. Her gathering basket bubbled over with flowers so that it looked as if she had just stepped out of a garden in full bloom.

Christy's round cheeks glowed. Her clear eyes danced, taking in the rose petals on the runner, the guests smiling along the aisles, and the bows and flowers strung along the way. Sierra watched as Christy looked up to the front of the church. Her eyes stopped their merry waltz when she saw the best man. Her gaze fixed on Todd, and she didn't seem to blink the rest of the way down the aisle.

Sierra smiled when she saw the expression on Todd's face. He seemed mesmerized by Christy's appearance. His mouth hung open slightly, and his eyes had grown wide and stayed fixed like that as he, too, didn't seem to blink.

In the pew two rows in front of Sierra sat Christy's parents and her younger brother. Bob sat next to him, and Marti was on the other side of Bob. She noticed both Christy's mom and dad dabbing at the corners of their eyes after their daughter floated past them.

Out of curiosity, Sierra glanced across the aisle at Rick. He sat a head taller than the young women who were perched on either side of him. His back was straight, his chin stuck out, and his lips were pursed together. One eyebrow was raised slightly. He wasn't taking his eyes off Christy either. Sierra decided she would have to ask Katie about this guy. If anyone could fill Sierra in, it would be Katie.

The piano music came to a sweeping finish as Christy took her place at the front. The organist picked up right where the piano ended. Grand and glorious, the music of the traditional wedding march boldly flew from the shiny organ pipes and filled the church. Tracy's mom stood and turned toward the entrance. The rest of the guests took her cue and stood as well. Sierra peeked at Doug. He straightened his shoulders and seemed to draw in a deep breath. Then his face lit up. Sierra knew Tracy had appeared in the doorway and had started down the aisle. Not because she saw Tracy, but because it was written all over Doug's face.

Now, that is the look of a man in love! Sierra thought, sighing. *He's about to burst. I think I even see tears in his eyes.*

Without warning, a fresh batch of tears sprang to

Sierra's eyes, blurring her vision. How could anyone keep from crying after seeing the expression on Doug's face? Sierra quickly wiped away her tears and turned to look at the bride.

Petite Tracy securely held her father's arm. Her dainty steps barely ruffled the rose petals strewn along her path. She was clothed in white from head to toe. Her dress had a delicate lace inset on the bodice, and the long sleeves were made of the same sheer lace. The full skirt was sprinkled with pearls and behind her flowed a long, satin train.

As magnificent as the dress was, it wasn't the gown that was most noticeable. What stood out more than anything was the radiance of Tracy's heart-shaped face beneath the thin veil of lace. The veil hung around her like a wisp of a cloud and seemed to tumble like a waterfall from the crownlike wreath of all white flowers that she wore so elegantly on the top of her head. In her hand, she held one long-stemmed white rose. Tracy was the picture of virtue and purity. To Sierra, she seemed to be a walking work of art. And the sight of her seemed to make everyone want to cry.

A rustling filled the church as the guests sat down.

The pastor spoke up. "Who gives this woman to be wedded to this man in holy matrimony?"

"Her mother and I," said Tracy's dad with a tremble in his voice.

He squeezed Tracy's hand. Doug stepped forward. Tracy's dad symbolically took Tracy's hand out of his and placed it into Doug's. Then he let go of her and went to the empty seat next to his wife.

Doug not only grasped Tracy's hand when it was given to him, but he also tucked her arm through his and pulled her close. Together they climbed the three small steps that led to the kneeling bench under the archway. The scene created a beautiful picture, the two of them standing there before God and the many witnesses. Sierra hoped with all her heart that one day her wedding would be this sacred and beautiful.

The pastor began by stating in a rich, rolling voice that marriage was a holy institution and not to be entered into lightly. He read Scripture and talked about the mystery of God's design in directing two people to be knit together in love.

"God's Word makes it clear that a man is to leave his mother and father and cleave to his wife. The two are to become one flesh. These are your instructions then," the pastor said. "You are to leave your parents, cleave to one another, and allow God to weave your lives together." He solemnly told Doug and Tracy that it would take every-thing in them and a strong relationship with Christ to make their marriage a lasting one.

"I now have instructions for you, the guests," the pastor said, looking beyond Doug and Tracy to their family and friends. "You are to pray for this young couple. Encourage them. Love them. Always expect the best from them and be ready in times of adversity to offer your support to them. I charge you to nurture this union."

He motioned for Tracy and Doug to kneel. Doug helped Tracy lower herself onto the soft kneeling bench. The minister stretched out his hand over the couple and prayed for them, for their marriage, and even for the children that might come from their union. Sierra silently agreed with the minister as he prayed for God's richest blessings on Doug and Tracy.

When they stood again, the minister instructed them to hold hands, face each other, and repeat their vows.

"I, Douglas Scott, take you, Tracy Lynn, as my lawfully wedded wife. I promise before God, our family, and our friends to love, honor, and cherish you until God takes me home to be with Him."

"I, Tracy Lynn, take you, Douglas Scott, as my lawfully wedded husband. I promise before God, our family, and our friends to love, honor, and cherish you until God takes me home to be with Him."

The pastor motioned for them to exchange the rings. Todd reached out his hand and placed the ring in Doug's open palm.

Looking into his bride's eyes, Doug lifted her left hand and slowly inched the ring onto her finger. "As a constant reminder of my never-ending love for you, I seal my vow with this ring."

Tracy turned to Christy. It appeared to Sierra that Christy was wearing Doug's large wedding band on her thumb, and now she easily slipped it off and handed it to Tracy.

Lifting Doug's hand, Tracy pushed the ring on and

repeated the words, "As a constant reminder of my never-ending love for you, I seal my vow with this ring."

The couple then turned to face the minister, and the piano played a gentle tune. A young man stood by the piano and sang into a handheld microphone a popular Christian love song that Sierra had heard once before at a wedding. As she listened, she looked down at her gold ring.

Father God, this ring is already becoming a constant reminder of Your never-ending love for me, she prayed silently. *I vow to stay pure and save myself for the man You want me to marry, and I seal my vow to You with this ring.*

She clasped her hands together in her lap and for the first time was glad her ring was gold and not silver. It symbolized something strong and powerful. Sierra liked that it didn't resemble all her other fun jewelry. This ring was special, just as Wes had said. It was set apart from all the rest. And in a way, at this moment, that's how she felt.

Chapter Eighteen

HE FINAL NOTE ESCAPED FROM THE SINGER'S throat. He returned to his seat, and all eyes returned to Doug and Tracy, who had stepped away from the arch, each on the appropriate side, and walked around until they met at the altar.

"In thanksgiving for their purity before God and between each other," the pastor said, "Doug and Tracy are offering a sacrifice of praise to the Lord. Each of them now presents a gift on the altar."

Tracy laid her long-stemmed white rose on top of the altar. Doug unpinned the white rose boutonniere from his lapel and laid it down. The pastor swung the kneeling bench out from under the arch so that it resembled a garden gate. Doug and Tracy joined hands and walked through the gate together. They stood just on the other side of the arch and looked intently into each other's eyes.

"By the power vested in me by the State of California and as a minister of the gospel of Christ the Risen Savior, I now pronounce you husband and wife."

There was a pause.

The minister smiled and said, "You may kiss your bride."

Sierra held her breath. It seemed as if the hundreds of well-wishers around her were doing the same thing. Out of the corner of her eye, Sierra saw Jeremy reach over and take Tawni's hand in his. They all sat perfectly still, waiting.

Doug carefully took the ends of Tracy's veil and lifted the sheer fabric over her head so that it tumbled down her back like fine mist from a waterfall. Tracy, with unveiled face, tilted her lips toward Doug and looked into his eyes.

He looked back at her. They acted as if they were oblivious to the hundreds of guests clinging to the edge of their pews and inwardly cheering, "Come on, kiss her!"

Doug took Tracy's sweet face in his large hands and whispered something to her. He tilted his head just right and slowly drew closer to her upturned face.

Then their lips met.

Sierra bit her lower lip and blinked fast to stop the tears from coming.

It was a long kiss. A slow kiss. A tender, unhurried, and wonderfully romantic kiss. Doug slowly drew away from Tracy and opened his eyes as if everything were in slow motion. A huge smile broke across his face, and Tracy let out a little giggle.

Someone broke loose with a "Bravo!" and sponta-neously, all around the sanctuary, friends and family were rising to their feet, clapping and cheering.

Doug turned to greet the outburst with a look of surprise. Tracy looked startled, too. And a little embarrassed. Then she started to laugh and motioned for Doug to look up in the balcony. Everyone turned to look. There stood the ushers in a straight row, holding up large, numbered cards that read: 10.0, 9.8, 9.9, 10.0, 10.0.

The church filled with bursts of laughter. The organ cranked up extra loud, and in the church steeple, bells began to ring. Tracy took Doug's arm, and with joyful tears rolling down their cheeks, they began their march down the center aisle. Everyone was standing, still clapping, still cheering, as the newlyweds hurried out the back door.

Todd and Christy followed them, smiling broadly and whispering to each other as they walked arm in arm across the crushed rose petals. It seemed to Sierra that they, too, were oblivious to the rest of the world and that they gave the appearance of floating rather than walking.

The rest of the party exited. The ushers came down from their judges' booth and began to dismiss the guests by undoing the ribbons and directing everyone down the center aisle, one row at a time.

The mood was the most festive Sierra had ever experienced at a church service or wedding. People were talking, laughing, and greeting each other with big hugs. Sierra followed Tawni and Jeremy out of the church. They were still holding hands and talking in a close way that indicated they wanted to be alone. As soon as Sierra was out of the church narthex, she took off ahead of Tawni and Jeremy as the guests all headed for the building where the reception was to be held.

As she entered the large gymnasium, Sierra thought

the decorating committee had done a pretty good job of dressing up the place. Dozens of small round tables were decorated with tablecloths of soft pink, lavender, and blue, just like the bridesmaids' dresses. Huge ferns hung from the basketball hoops. The three-tiered cake graced the center of the long serving table. Sierra noticed that it was holding its shape quite nicely. Marti would be relieved that it hadn't crumbled in the August heat.

In the far corner was a white-carpeted area with a decorated archway woven with ivy and bright summer flowers. Sierra guessed that that was to be the receiving line. She couldn't wait to give Doug and Tracy her best wishes. But it would probably be awhile before they formed the line, since more pictures were being taken.

Finding an empty table, Sierra sat down and tried one of the pastel mints in a dish next to a vase of fresh flowers. Katie made her way over to the table and leaned on her crutches.

"Was that a wedding to remember, or what?" Katie slid the crutches under the table, and Sierra pulled out a chair for her. "Did you see their kiss? Of course you did. Everyone did. I didn't know the guys were going to do the numbers up in the balcony. What a scream!"

Katie's flushed face matched her red hair. She sat down and said, "Man, I'm pooped from trying to get around on this stupid foot. I can't believe I have to wear this cast for a month. This is so pathetic."

Sierra noticed Rick pulling out a chair for a slender brunette a few tables over.

"Katie, who is that guy?"

Katie looked over her shoulder and, with wide eyes, leaned toward Sierra and said, "Don't go there, Sierra. Trust me on this one. Stay far away from him."

"I don't think you have to worry about that. He's the one who wants to stay far away from me." Sierra told Katie about her exchange with Rick and how he had gotten up and moved right before the ceremony started.

Katie started to laugh and said, "I wish I'd been more like you a few years ago." She shook her head.

"You didn't date that guy, did you?" Sierra said.

"If you could call it that. He was my first kiss. Can you believe that? What was I thinking?"

Sierra was amazed.

"Actually, that's a dumb question. I know what I was thinking. I was thinking, if he's good enough for Christy to kiss, then why can't I kiss him, too?"

"You aren't serious," Sierra said, her eyebrows coming closer together as she scrutinized Katie's expression. "Not our Christy! Christy Miller? She didn't go out with that guy . . . did she?"

Katie nodded.

"And she kissed him?"

Katie leaned forward across the table, nearly toppling the bowl of mints. "Let me just say, Sierra, that you need to understand that with Rick, he is the kisser and you are the kissee. I don't know that I could say that Christy ever initiated a kiss with him; but yes, he did kiss her quite a few times. He was crazy about her. She was like this unattainable prize to him. I'll admit it; I was jealous of her. So when Christy broke up with Rick, and he showed a little interest in me, of course I gobbled it up."

Sierra still had a hard time imagining that both of these friends, whom she deeply admired, had ever given any part of themselves to a guy like Rick. He seemed like an incurable flirt to Sierra.

"Oh, the things we do when we're young and stupid," Katie said, leaning back and shaking her silky red hair. "If it weren't for the grace of God, we would all be a sad bunch of losers, wouldn't we?"

Sierra nodded slowly. She was thinking of Amy. "So how did you figure out that you shouldn't be investing your kisses in Rick?"

"Investing my kisses," Katie repeated. "I like that. I don't know. It just all fell apart. There wasn't anything to hold it together. Then I fell in love with Michael. You remember my telling you about him in England."

"He was the exchange student you stopped going out with because he wasn't a Christian, right?"

Katie nodded. "That one was really hard. We were together for a long time. It still hurts when I think about him. Christy was such a great friend to me during that time, though. Right away she told me exactly what she thought of us getting together, and then she let me live my own life, even though she thought I was making a huge mistake."

"Do you think it was a mistake to go out with Michael?"

Katie paused. Then, curling up her lower lip, she said,

"Yeah, I guess looking back it wasn't the wisest choice. I emotionally poured a lot of myself out. You know, I kept praying for him and talking to him about the Lord. I was so sure he would 'see the light,' as they say. It cost me a lot inside—in my heart, where it really counts."

"But you said Christy didn't try to persuade you not to get involved with him. Weren't you close friends?"

"Oh, the best! I think Christy did the right thing. She told me what she thought, and I know she prayed long and hard for me, but then she let me go my own way and just continued to be a consistent friend through it all. Then, when I crashed and burned, she was right there to salvage the wreckage."

Katie's glance moved past Sierra to someone standing behind her. Katie's green eyes flashed a look of delight as she practically shouted, "You came!"

Sierra turned to see Antonio, a guy from Italy whom she had met on the beach last Easter. Sparks had flown between Katie and Antonio then, and obviously that interest was still alive inside of Katie.

"I heard you are a movie star." Antonio's rich accent washed over both of them. "Something about a cast of thousands." He stepped over to where Katie had planted herself and leaned down to kiss her lightly on each side of her face.

"Only one cast, Tonio," Katie said, her eyes still gleaming. "And it's on my foot."

"Tsk, tsk, tsk," Antonio said, shaking his head and clucking his tongue in a way that was decidedly European.

"This is such a pity. I was hoping you would go water-skiing with me tomorrow."

"I can still sit in the boat and hold up the flag," Katie said.

Antonio laughed. Then he turned to see who was sitting with Katie.

"Sierra! I did not know it was you."

He bent over, and before she knew what he was doing, he brushed his lips faintly against the side of each of her cheeks. She immediately felt herself blushing.

Behind them a surge of voices rose, along with cheers and applause.

"It looks as if the bride and groom have finally arrived," Antonio said. "Come with me, Katie, Sierra. Let's get in their giving line." He held out an arm for each of them.

"Tonio," Katie corrected him, rising with the help of his strong arm, "it's a receiving line, not a giving line."

"For you, perhaps. For me, it is a giving line. I'm giving the bride a kiss."

Chapter Nineteen

STANDING IN THE LONG LINE BEHIND KATIE AND Antonio gave Sierra a chance to think. So many things had impressed her during the past few hours. The emotionally powerful ceremony had awakened a new sense of longing within her. It wasn't just a desire to be loved deeply someday by a man like Doug; it was a sense of responsibility to prepare now for that man.

She remembered what the pastor had said about God's mysterious design in directing two people to be knit together in love. It was all a mystery to her. She was sure the only way to navigate a marriage relationship was the same way she should be handling her dating years now—by praying hard and trusting God each step of the way.

What Katie had said a few minutes ago at the table had helped her decide what to do about Amy. Sierra now knew that it wasn't her responsibility to change her friend's heart and mind. Only God could do that. She could certainly state her opinions loudly and clearly, and she had never had a problem doing that. But Sierra needed to learn from Christy's example by standing back and simply praying for her best friend.

Antonio stepped out of the line.

Katie smiled at Sierra. "He's going to get me some punch. Is that guy the ultimate gentleman, or what?"

"I like him, too," Sierra said.

"You do?" Katie's countenance fell.

"Not like that," Sierra said, laughing at Katie's expression. "I mean, I think he's a great guy. I know he has a deep love for the Lord and that makes him . . ."

"Irresistible." Katie finished the sentence for her.

They both laughed. The line inched forward. Sierra brushed the curls off the side of her neck.

"Is that a purity ring?" Katie asked, eyeing the gold band.

"Yes. My dad gave it to me last week. After watching Doug and Tracy place their roses on the altar, I have to admit, I was ready to start a nationwide purity campaign."

"It's already been done," Katie said.

"I know. But you know what I mean. If more of my friends had examples like Doug and Tracy, I think they would be more deliberate about who they date and about saving themselves for marriage."

"You're right," Katie agreed. "I bought myself a ring." She held up her right hand and showed Sierra the simple, silver-twisted band. "My parents aren't Christians, so I wasn't expecting my dad to surprise me with a father-daughter bonding moment or hand me a little velvet box and everything."

A lump caught in Sierra's throat. She did have a Christian dad, who had gone to the effort of making their dinner a special occasion. He had handed her the little velvet box. And all she could think of that night was how embarrassed she was.

I wish I had worn the corsage. I wish I would have been more appreciative, she thought.

"Some of my friends went to those nationwide campaigns while they were in high school," Katie said. "They signed cards or something, and their whole youth group got rings to wear. Our youth group somehow missed out on all that. Or maybe they went, and I didn't go for some reason. Anyway, I decided to make my own purity vow. So I bought this ring and took myself to the beach one morning really early. I sat on this big rock and read my Bible and sang and then put on the ring."

Just then Antonio returned with the punch.

"Here you are," Antonio said, handing a glass to Katie and one to Sierra. "I see we're almost to the front of the line. Good work, ladies."

Within three short minutes, they had reached the reception line and were shaking hands with a string of Doug's and Tracy's relatives and the wedding party and congratulating them all. Sierra received a hug from Todd and then a crushing hug from Doug. He was still looking happier than any man alive should be allowed to look.

Sierra kissed Tracy on the cheek. She had to. Tracy looked so beautiful that a hug wasn't enough. And it wasn't enough for Antonio either. He soundly kissed Tracy on both cheeks and pronounced an Italian blessing on the couple.

Sierra then gave Christy a hug and told her how beautiful she looked.

"Not only beautiful," Antonio said, overhearing Sierra's comment. "Christina, you are radiant. I predict you will catch the croquet."

"Not the croquet," Katie said, playfully swatting at Antonio's arm. "The bouquet."

"Oh. It is not long-handled wooden mallets you Americans throw at your guests?"

Katie seemed to come alive around Antonio and gobbled up his teasing. "No, it is not long-handled wooden mallets," Katie repeated in her best imitative Italian accent. "It's long-stemmed, fragrant flowers."

"No!" Antonio said in mock surprise. "Once again you have shown me that I would be lost without your instruction in this strange land in which I sojourn." He slipped his arm around Katie's shoulder.

"The only strange land in which you sojourn, Tonio, is your own mind," Katie teased.

He shot right back. "And you would know this, because you have been there."

"Been where?"

"In my mind."

"Actually, instead of *in*, we say *on my mind*," Katie began.

Then it seemed to dawn on her that he had given her a

sweet compliment. Sierra suspected she was watching another budding romance among her friends. Now she truly was the odd one. The young one. The unattached one. The one in the "adorable" yellow dress.

Sierra sat quietly with all her friends—the couples—and did some thinking.

Nearly an hour later, Tracy threw the bouquet. All the eligible young women gathered outside the church for the big moment.

"It's a fake, you know," Katie said. "Tracy carried a single white rose, remember? This bouquet is for tradition's sake."

"I still think it's a wonderful tradition," Tawni said, taking her place next to Sierra. It almost appeared she was placing herself at the best probable angle to catch the bouquet.

The photographer snapped a couple of shots, while all the guys stood to the side, cheering for their favorite. Christy was, of course, the most adored candidate. On the count of three, Tracy tossed the bouquet over her shoulder and high into the air.

Sierra looked up into the summer evening sky and realized it was coming right toward her. With a leap, she could snatch it. But something deep inside her spoke. Not a voice, really, but more than a thought. Clearer than a feeling.

Wait.

Sierra didn't leap. Tawni stretched her long, limber arms and snatched the bouquet. The joy of her victory was immediately evident. She waved the bouquet in the direction of all the guys, and they began to rough up Jeremy, telling him that now the pressure was on to catch the garter.

Tracy lifted her gown only slightly, revealing the fancy lace garter around the middle of her calf. Teasing comments about her modesty pelted Doug as he removed the garter. The eligible and not-so-eligible guys lined up, pushing and joking.

Without much warning, Doug turned his back to the rowdy bunch and said, "Here it comes!"

The elastic garter shot straight into the air, and like a bunch of pro basketball players, the guys all leaped to catch it. Not until the huddle of men peeled themselves off each other were they able to see who had caught the garter.

"Rick Doyle?" Christy spouted. Her face seemed to turn a little gray. "I didn't know he was here," she whispered to Katie.

Sierra wanted to say, "Well, Rick sure knew you were," but she decided to leave that one alone. Apparently, Christy's memories of this guy were not exactly heart-warming.

Tawni and Rick posed for the photographer. Sierra noticed how perfectly Tawni stood and smiled, her head at just the right angle. She was a natural in front of the camera.

"Here, take a handful," a woman said, thrusting a big bag of birdseed in front of Sierra. "Instead of rice," she explained. "It's organic."

As Sierra grabbed from the bag, a white Rolls Royce pulled up in front of the church, complete with a chauffeur wearing a black cap. He got out and opened the car's back door. Tracy kissed her mom and dad good-bye and then linked her arm in Doug's as they merrily dashed for the get-away car.

"Now!" the lady with the birdseed called out.

Doug and Tracy were showered with thousands of tiny bits of birdseed that their cheering friends tossed in the air. Tracy lifted her long skirt slightly as she slid into the Rolls's backseat. Doug held the long train for her and then ducked his way in beside her. The chauffeur shut the door and walked calmly around to the driver's side as if he did this every day.

"Bye. Have fun! See you," everyone called out.

"Where are they going on their honeymoon?" Sierra asked.

"Maui," said Tawni. "Didn't you know? They're going to Bob and Marti's condo."

"Sierra," Jeremy said. "I started to tell you something right before the ceremony."

"Oh, yes." She had forgotten.

Jeremy gave Tawni a smile, and taking Sierra's elbow, he led her away from the crowd to an open spot on the church lawn.

"It's about my brother," Jeremy said. "I think you should write to him."

"Why?"

"Well, it's just that he's . . ."

"Is he okay? I mean, he isn't in trouble or dying or anything, is he?"

"No, Paul is doing great. Really great, actually. Better than ever. I honestly think you've had a lot to do with that."

"Me? How?"

"I know you've been praying for him. But it's more than that. Here. I don't know how to tell you any other way."

Jeremy pulled a piece of paper from his pocket and unfolded it. Sierra immediately recognized the bold, dark letters of Paul's distinctive handwriting.

"Right here," Jeremy said, pointing to the last paragraph. "He's talking about going on these walks in the highlands of Scotland where my grandmother lives, and then he says . . . well, you read it."

Sierra took the letter and read aloud: "'You'll probably laugh, but the face I keep seeing in the clouds above this "bonnie" land is Sierra's. Last June, in Portland, I thought I could pat her on the head and send her out of my mind. But look. She's followed me here. She told me God has put His mark on my life. Do you think that's true? What does it mean? What does God want me to do with my life?'"

Stunned, Sierra looked at Jeremy and said the first thing that came to her mind. "These are Paul's private thoughts. I don't think he meant for you to show them to me."

"Maybe not, but don't you see? He needs some encouragement right now, and I think it should come from you."

Something deep within Sierra spoke to her again. Not a voice or a thought. Clearer than a feeling.

Wait.

In that moment, it didn't matter to Sierra that she was the youngest or the only one without a boyfriend. It didn't even matter that she was wearing Christy's yellow dress. She was finally beginning to recognize her true identity. Bob's quote from Augustine came back to her: "For He alone who made thee in His image can satisfy thee."

Reverently, Sierra folded the piece of paper. The gold band on her right hand caught the light as she handed Paul's letter back to Jeremy.

"This may sound overly simple," Sierra said, "but I believe God will meet Paul right where he is. And God's the only One who can answer questions like these."

Jeremy looked at her for a moment, his handsome face expressionless. Then he said, "I think Paul would like to get a letter from you."

"Maybe he would," Sierra said. Then, with a smile and a pat on Jeremy's broad shoulder, she added, "Tell him to write me first."

With a swish of the yellow dress, she turned and headed back to join the others. Sierra felt full of hope and confidence in God. She knew who she was. And she knew Whose she was.

Whatever mysterious plan God had for her life, it would be an interesting one. As Christy had said earlier, God writes a different story for each person. Sierra decided hers may not be a best-seller or even a thriller. It certainly wasn't a romance. But it was turning into a fine mystery. And she could live with that.

FOCUS ON THE FAMILY®
*L*IKE THIS BOOK?

Then you'll love *Brio* magazine! Written especially for teen girls, it's packed each month with 32 pages on everything from fiction and faith to fashion, food . . . even guys! Best of all, it's all from a Christian perspective! But don't just take our word for it. Instead, see for yourself by requesting a complimentary copy.

Simply write Focus on the Family, Colorado Springs, CO 80995 (in Canada, write P.O. Box 9800, Stn. Terminal, Vancouver, B.C. V6B 4G3) and mention that you saw this offer in the back of this book. You may also call 1-800-232-6459 (in Canada, call 1-800-661-9800).

You may also visit our Web site (www.family.org) to learn more about the ministry or find out if there is a Focus on the Family office in your country.

Want to become everyone's favorite baby-sitter? Then *The Ultimate Baby-Sitter's Survival Guide* is for you! It's packed with page after page of practical information and ways to stay in control; organize mealtime, bath time and bedtime; and handle emergency situations. It also features an entire section of safe, creative and downright crazy indoor and outdoor activities that will keep kids challenged, entertained and away from the television. Easy-to-read and reference, it's the ideal book for providing the best care to children, earning money and having fun at the same time.

Call Focus on the Family at the number above, or check out your local Christian bookstore.

Focus on the Family is an organization that is dedicated to helping you and your family establish lasting, loving relationships with each other and the Lord. It's why we exist! If we can assist you or your family in any way, please feel free to contact us. We'd love to hear from you!

Don't Miss These Captivating Stories in
THE SIERRA JENSEN SERIES

The Christy Miller Series

If you've enjoyed reading about Sierra Jensen, you'll love reading about Sierra's friend Christy Miller. She seems like a real-life friend that you can relate to, trust, and get to know.

#1 • Summer Promise
Christy spends the summer at the beach with her wealthy aunt and uncle. Will she do something she'll later regret?

#2 • A Whisper and a Wish
Christy is convinced that dreams do come true when her family moves to California and the cutest guy in school shows an interest in her.

#3 • Yours Forever
Fifteen-year-old Christy does everything in her power to win Todd's attention.

#4 • Surprise Endings
Christy tries out for cheerleader, learns a classmate is out to get her, and schedules two dates for the same night.

#5 • Island Dreamer
It's an incredible tropical adventure when Christy celebrates her sixteenth birthday on Maui.

#6 • A Heart Full of Hope
A dazzling dream date, a wonderful job, a great car. And lots of freedom! Christy has it all. Or does she?

#7 • True Friends
Christy sets out with the ski club and discovers the group is thinking of doing something more than hitting the slopes.

#8 • Starry Night
Christy is torn between going to the Rose Bowl Parade with her friends or on a surprise vacation with her family.

#9 • Seventeen Wishes
Christy is off to summer camp—as a counselor for a cabin of wild fifth-grade girls.

#10 • A Time to Cherish
A surprise houseboat trip! Her senior year! Lots of friends! Life couldn't be better for Christy until . . .

#11 • Sweet Dreams
Christy's dreams become reality when Todd finally opens his heart to her. But her relationship with her best friend goes downhill fast when Katie starts dating Michael, and Christy has doubts about their relationship.

#12 • A Promise Is Forever
On a European trip with her friends, Christy finds it difficult to keep her mind off Todd. Will God bring them back together?

9803